"You are going to marry me, Leonie."

"No," she whispered, her eyes held hypnotically by the power of his demanding stare. "I couldn't marry you. I can't even bear it when you touch me!"

As soon as the words left her lips she wished she could call them back; she knew it had been a stupid, reckless thing to say, and his expression underlined her own instincts.

"Can't you? Well, let's see, shall we?" Giles bit out, and her nerves leapt at the furious flash of his icy gray eyes.

His mouth took hers with driving force.

CHARLOTTE LAMB is one of Harlequin's best-loved and bestselling authors. Her extraordinary career, in which she has written more than one hundred books, has helped shape the face of romance fiction around the world.

Born in the East End of London, Charlotte spent her early childhood moving from relative to relative to escape the bombings of World War II. After working as a secretary in the BBC's European department, she married a political reporter who wrote for the *Times*. Charlotte recalls that it was at his suggestion that she began to write "because it was one job I could do without having to leave our five children." Charlotte and her family now live in a beautiful home on the Isle of Man. It is the perfect setting for an author who creates characters and stories that delight romance readers everywhere.

Books by Charlotte Lamb

Charlotte Lamb

FORBIDDEN FRUIT

Harlequin Books

TORONTO • NEW YORK • LONDON
AMSTERDAM • PARIS • SYDNEY • HAMBURG
STOCKHOLM • ATHENS • TOKYO • MILAN
MADRID • WARSAW • BUDAPEST • AUCKLAND

Harlequin Presents Plus first edition September 1993
ISBN 0-373-11584-9

Original hardcover edition published in 1991
by Mills & Boon Limited

FORBIDDEN FRUIT

CHAPTER ONE

LEONIE craned her neck to catch sight of herself in the mirror, and caught her breath, her lips parting in an audible gasp. She didn't recognise the slender girl in the floating white dress; it was a stranger standing there. Oh, she knew the silvery fair hair which she often wished less fine, the oval face it framed, the skin she always felt was too pale, the widely spaced dark blue eyes. Her familiar features looked back at her, sure enough; and yet there was a disorientating sense of unfamiliarity. Could a dress make that much difference?

'That isn't me!' she thought aloud, and Angela impatiently clicked her tongue.

'Stand still, or I won't be able to get the hem straight!'

'Sorry!' Leonie obediently lapsed back into her previous posture, looking out through the window into a cold blue sky. It was early spring; a chill wind lashed the trees along the London street, but there were daffodils braving the wintry afternoon and pink sprays of blossom breaking out on the almond tree's black boughs.

'So Malcolm's away for three more days?' asked Angela, deftly inserting a final pin in the hem and leaning back to assess the result.

She had insisted that the dress should be her wedding present to the bride, even refusing to let Leonie pay for the beautiful and expensive materials, the silk, ribbon and lace. The style was romantic in the extreme; extravagantly medieval, a high-necked, long-sleeved gown which made the girl in it look like the heroine of a fairy-story come to life.

Leonie knew that Angela's work was so good that she had a long waiting list of clients, to whom she charged very high rates.

'It's too generous of you!' she had protested when Angela first said she was going to make the wedding dress as her present to the bride, but Angela had simply brushed the words aside with a shake of the head.

'Don't argue, I've made up my mind!' she had said firmly. Angela prided herself on being down to earth. Warm-hearted she might be, but she hated to be emotional.

Leonie's mouth curved in a smile now. 'Yes, Malcolm gets back on Thursday.'

'He goes away a lot, doesn't he?'

Leonie's smile faltered. 'Lately he does, yes. He never used to, but I think his brother is deliberately sending him on all these selling trips to keep him away from me.' Her blue eyes were shadowed now, and she looked down at her friend unhappily. 'If they could stop Malcolm marrying me, they would, you know. They don't think I'm good enough for him.'

Angela bristled indignantly, and stood up, her face flushed. 'Are they still being standoffish with you? Who do they think they are? Royalty?'

Leonie gave a husky laugh. 'I wouldn't be surprised! They are very wealthy, Angela. The firm has been making paper at Kent Warlock Mills since the nineteenth century, and their home is much older than that, although I think they bought it about fifty years ago. They haven't always lived at Warlock House, but Mrs Kent comes from a very old family. She grew up in a castle somewhere in Scotland.'

Angela snorted, unimpressed. 'That doesn't give her the right to look down on you! I've no time for snobs.'

Angela was always very forthright; a short, determined brunette with fierce brown eyes and lots of energy. She and Leonie were opposites in many ways and yet they had been friends since they were at school, perhaps because something vulnerable in Leonie's nature made Angela feel she needed someone to look after her and tell her what to do, and Angela was good at that.

Nobody was ever going to get the chance of ordering Angela about, of course, which was why, when she started work, her passion for dressmaking had quite naturally led to her setting up in business on her own. She was successful from the start, and she was her own boss. The job enabled her to work from home, independently, doing as much, or as little, each day, as she chose.

'I can understand Mrs Kent's being disappointed that Malcolm isn't marrying someone from her own background,' Leonie said soberly, trying to be fair, and Angela made impatient noises.

'Someone with money, you mean!'

'I really don't think it is just a question of money. They wanted Malcolm to marry a different sort of girl. Someone from their world, someone whose family they know. I'm just a secretary from an ordinary family.'

'They should be glad Malcolm has found someone so pretty and nice,' Angela said aggressively, and Leonie smiled at her.

'Thanks. Oh, I expect they'll get used to the idea of me. I'll do my best to fit in, and, after all, Malcolm and I have known each other for nine months; they must realise we're both serious. It isn't a spur of the moment impulse—we know what we're doing. I only hope they come to the wedding . . .'

Angela looked shocked. 'You mean, they might not come?'

'Malcolm says they will, but they haven't answered the invitations my mother sent them.'

'Well, if they don't come they aren't worth bothering about. This is going to be your big day, so don't let them spoil it for you! Once you and Malcolm are married they'll soon come round, wait and see.'

'Do you think so?' Leonie's delicate face lit up, and Angela nodded firmly.

'Of course. There is one thing you can always be sure about with rich people—they're realists. Once you're Malcolm's wife they'll come to terms with the idea.' She caught sight of the clock on the mantelshelf, and gave a groan. 'Look at the time! I've got to meet Jack in the West End at six—we're going to a party. I haven't got time to take the dress home first. I'll have to leave it here, and pick it up tomorrow morning—but guard it with your life. I want it to be perfect on the day!'

'You don't need to worry.'

'But I do!' Angela began hurrying to the door, but lingered, her anxious eyes on the dress. 'Maybe I should stay and help you take it off?'

'I can do it!'

'Well, OK, but . . . you will be extra careful, especially with the zip?'

'Of course!'

'And don't, whatever you do, let Malcolm see it; it's unlucky!'

'I won't be seeing him!'

'No, of course not.' Angela still couldn't tear herself away. 'And put it back inside the cover before you hang it up!' she reminded her from the door.

'I know!' Leonie laughed and made pushing gestures. 'Go on! I can manage!'

Laughing, Angela said, 'OK. Bye, then, see you tomorrow!' She vanished, the front door of the little flat slammed, and Leonie turned slowly to stare once again at her own reflection, able to do so, this time, at her leisure. She was thrilled with her dress and the way it made her look— she couldn't wait for Malcolm to see it. She had so badly wanted to look really special on their wedding-day, and Angela's clever fingers were going to make that dream come true. Nobody else would ever have had precisely this style of dress, since Angela had designed it for her, a unique, one-off wedding dress for her day in a lifetime.

This was how she had dreamt of looking—so why did she feel strange, unfamiliar?

A frown knit her brows. She was passionately in love with Malcolm—it couldn't be any doubts about him—but she had to face it. Her wedding-day was not going to be all bliss, nor could she be certain about her future life with the man she loved, which was why her moods, for weeks, had swung wildly between deep happiness and a troubled uneasiness. Oh, not about Malcolm, or their feelings for each other—but about his family's hostility, and how that might affect their relationship.

From the very beginning the Kent family had made no secret of their shock, and their dislike of the girl Malcolm had taken home to meet them one hot July evening. She remembered it as if it had been yesterday. There had been thunderstorms rumbling somewhere in the distance, across the rolling wheatfields in the Essex farmland surrounding Warlock House. The sky had been an ominous colour; heavy with cloud, an occasional flash of lightning splitting the horizon. Midges had hummed under the heavy green branches of the trees in the beautifully kept gardens, and the air had been humid.

Leonie had noticed all that, anxiously, and then had been struck dumb by the magnificence of Malcolm's home, a large Queen Anne house built of red brick and stone, set in parkland. The interior matched the beauty and grace of the façade: golden oak panelling, polished woodblock floors, gleaming antique furniture and flowers everywhere, scenting the rooms.

She had become so nervous by the time she met Malcolm's family that she was trembling as she shook hands with Mrs Kent, a slim, elegant woman with silvered dark hair. Leonie knew she had been widowed for some five years, and was over sixty, but she certainly did not look it.

Face to face, Leonie had shakily smiled, but been given no smile in reply. Mrs Kent had merely looked Leonie up and down, her thin brows rising in cold disdain.

Meeting those dagger-sharp grey eyes, Leonie had hurriedly turned away to shake hands with Malcolm's elder brother, Giles, only to face the same animosity, the same icily level gaze, and to recognise with a sinking heart that there was no welcome for her in that house.

In the ensuing weeks they had made sure that she met some of the girls Malcolm might have married if he had not met her. They were much the same, all of them: rich, pretty, arrogant, fitting in perfectly with the world Malcolm's family inhabited. The Kent family wanted her to feel inferior and out of place, and Leonie was so shy and unsure of herself that she was an easy target.

One autumn evening she had stood alone at a garden barbecue at the Kent house, miserably watching Malcolm dancing with another girl, who had clung to him, her body sinuously moving in rhythm with his, her arms tightly clasping his neck. Leonie had felt like crying, but she had gritted her teeth and pretended to smile. After all, Malcolm had chosen her, hadn't he? He had not asked any of these other girls to marry him!

'Enjoying yourself?' Giles Kent had asked in a dry, sarcastic voice, suddenly joining her, and she had started, her body tense as she'd looked up at him. He rarely spoke to her, but when from time to time they did meet she always felt wary and tense in his company.

'Yes, thank you,' she had lied, and his mouth had twisted wryly.

'You don't look as if you are.'

'I can't help the way I look!' she had retorted, stung, and he had smiled with an odd sort of irony.

'No, I suppose you can't.' His grey eyes had flicked over her, and for no reason she could explain she had felt her skin burning. His face still held hostility, but for that second she had seen something else in his glance, a sensual awareness of her that had made her blush.

He had laughed at her hot colour. 'Did you think I hadn't noticed the way you look?' he'd softly mocked. 'I'm sure men always do. You're lovely, and I can't blame Malcolm for wanting you. I wouldn't say no, myself, if an offer was made.'

She would have been insulted if she had not been so startled. It was the last thing she had expected from Giles Kent, that sort of remark. She'd almost believed she was imagining the whole thing; hallucinating.

Then he had put out his hand and touched her neck, softly, lightly, his fingertips stroking downwards from her ear to her bare shoulder, and she had felt a shudder run right through her. The brief touch had had an intimacy that had shaken her like an earthquake. She had leapt backwards, eyes huge in her burning face, and a second later Malcolm had been there, frowning, looking at his elder brother with suspicion.

'What's going on? What are you up to, Giles?'

Coolly, Giles had drawled, 'I was making a pass at your girlfriend.'

She hadn't known where to look. Why was he acting this way? Was he trying to cause trouble? Insulting her? Trying to come between her and Malcolm? She could not believe he really felt any attraction; he had always been so icily hostile to her in the past.

Malcolm had stared at him, dark red colour rising in his face. 'Oh, you were, were you?'

The brothers had faced each other, their bodies tense as if they might come to blows any minute, and Leonie had been frightened. 'Stop it! Please, stop it!' she had cried, turning white. Malcolm had given her a quick, concerned look, and relaxed a little, grimacing.

'OK, darling, don't look so upset! I won't punch him in the nose, although he deserves it.'

'Let's go, Malcolm,' she had muttered, careful not to look at Giles.

Malcolm hadn't been ready to leave yet, though. He was too angry. 'Of course,' he'd said furiously, 'I might have known he would, sooner or later. He's used to women falling over themselves to get his attention; he probably thought he could have you with one snap of his fingers.'

Giles had stood there impassively, his face totally without expression, but every line of it taut, his bones locked in tense concentration.

Malcolm had laughed shortly. 'That's what you thought, isn't it, Giles? Well, you won't get anywhere with her—you can't stop our wedding that way! And you can tell Mother that she won't get anywhere with her delaying tactics, either. I'm not interested in any other girls, so tell her to stop pushing them at me. Whether she likes it or not, I love Leonie, and she loves me, and we are getting married, so you and Mother had better get used to the idea.'

Leonie had felt her heart turn over. At that moment she had really begun to believe she and Malcolm could be happy together, that it wasn't just an impossible dream. She had always been afraid that his family would lure him away from her, that his feelings for her would not last, but as he'd smiled down at her at that moment she had been so happy that she had almost burst into tears.

Remembering that evening, the smoky firelit garden, the music and laughter in the background, Giles Kent watching her with those remote grey eyes, and Malcolm smiling at her with love and reassurance, she sighed, a little smile curving her mouth. They were going to be happy. Whatever anyone said or did, in just a few days they would get married, and they would start to build a wonderful life together.

Dreamily, she turned away from the mirror and began to unhook the neck of her dress. A zip ran all the way down to the waist, at the back, but first she had to open the high neck. As she freed the hook she heard the doorbell begin to ring, and grinned to herself.

It was probably Angela, having changed her mind about leaving the precious dress here overnight. Leonie held her long skirts carefully in both hands, to lift the hem off the floor, and made her way to the front door.

Half laughing, she opened it, ready to tease her friend. It wasn't Angela outside, though. It was a tall man in a dark suit. Giles Kent!

Leonie's smile died; she stiffened at the first sight of him, her blue eyes startled.

'Oh. It's you,' she muttered, looking away immediately. It troubled her, as always, to meet his cool stare. He had known her for months now, but she was beginning to think that he would never like her, and yet at the same time she was always conscious of that underlying awareness of her, which he had first let her glimpse that day at the barbecue, an awareness matched inside herself, in spite of herself. It was far from being simple attraction; it was too complex for that; a disturbing mixture of hostility and a physical response, which she resisted angrily. She did not want to be conscious of that tall, lean body. She disliked the man intensely! Why on earth should she nevertheless feel this quiver of sensual attention whenever she saw him? She could only think that her dislike was so intense that it triggered off a chemical reaction that was far too much like desire.

She hoped he wasn't aware of her secret feelings, but something in those mocking grey eyes usually made her uneasily suspect he was. Not today, though. She frowned. Today, he was even more hostile than usual. He was frowning heavily, his mouth tightly controlled. Why was he looking at her like that? What was he doing here if he disliked her so much? Through her lashes she noted inconsequentially that he was wearing a black tie. Maybe he had been to a funeral? That would explain his grim expression—but not what he was doing here, visiting her. He had never been to her flat before. Why was he here now?

'What do you want?' she asked edgily.

He didn't answer; the sight of her in her wedding dress seemed to have stupefied him. That would have been the last thing he'd expected—to have her open the door to him in her wedding dress. No doubt he wondered why on earth she was wearing it!

'I was having a fitting,' she stumblingly explained.

'Oh, I see.' He seemed to wrench his stare from her, scowling, as though he hated the sight of her in the lace and silk dress.

He probably did. It must remind him that any day now she would be his sister-in-law, one of his family. Like his mother, Giles Kent did not think she was good enough for that.

'Are you alone?' he asked tersely, looking past her into the flat. Did he wonder if Malcolm was there? No, of course, he knew his brother was abroad on the firm's business, in Switzerland.

'Yes,' she admitted warily, wondering if she should refuse to let him enter her flat. Would it be wise to be alone with him? Malcolm had warned her, after that incident at the barbecue, not to trust his brother, never to let Giles near her. 'He's ruthless with women,' he had told her. 'Giles is ruthless with business, the family, everyone, but especially with women.'

Why was he here, when he knew his brother was away? She bit her lip, wondering what to do. 'Angela . . . the friend who is making my dress has just gone out,' she hurriedly said, rather flushed. 'But she should be back some time soon . . .'

He nodded again, but absently. 'May I come in?' He didn't wait for an answer. He stepped forward, and she had to let him pass. She wished she knew why he was here—she couldn't believe this was a casual, friendly visit. Had he come to ask her to give Malcolm up? To persuade? Or to threaten? The latter, probably; Giles Kent gave off an air of threat most of the time, and that was what she could expect from him.

Leonie felt stupid in the long, elaborately romantic dress and would have gone to take it off, except that she did not want to encourage Giles Kent to stay any longer than necessary. He made her far too nervous.

'Have you got any brandy?' he asked abruptly, swinging to face her suddenly, and she couldn't stop herself visibly flinching.

'B . . . brandy?' She looked rather wildly around the sitting-room, shaking her head.

'Sorry, I'm afraid...I don't drink, you see. I don't keep spirits in the flat. There is some white wine in the fridge, for dinner when Malcolm gets back——'

'He won't be back!' Giles Kent interrupted, his voice harsh, and she stared at him in some confusion, her brow furrowed.

'Is this trip taking longer than expected?'

Suspicion raced through her—were they trying to keep Malcolm abroad as long as possible, still hoping to separate them?

Giles didn't answer. Instead, he suddenly took her shoulders and pushed her backwards on to a chair. She was too surprised to struggle, her body pliant in his grip for a second. He looked so odd that he frightened her. He was going to make another pass at her, after all. Her heart beat suffocatingly, and she tried to think what to do. This time they were alone and she didn't know if she could handle him; he was so much stronger, a tall, hard, lean man whose body could dominate hers without much effort.

He bent over her, his face inches away, a disturbing mask of bone out of which grey eyes watched her frowningly.

'Please, don't...' she stammered, trembling, too scared even to be angry, but then he interrupted her, his voice rough.

'Leonie, listen ... God, I don't know how to say this ... there's no painless way of doing it— if I could, I would, but ... best to be quick, get it over.' He took a long breath. 'He's been killed.'

Leonie stared at him, blank-faced, not yet understanding. 'Who are you talking about?'

'Malcolm,' Giles said. 'Malcolm is dead.'

The breath seemed to leave her body. Her heart seemed to stop beating. She didn't make a sound, just sat there, staring.

Giles talked on in that angry voice, the words like bullets aimed at her, or fate, or maybe even himself. 'This morning—he was killed this morning. On the ski slopes. He came down too fast, collided with someone and was killed instantly, a head injury, a glancing blow from the other man's ski as they fell together. A one in a million chance, they say. A stupid accident, need not have happened if he had been thinking what he was doing ...'

Leonie hadn't moved, hadn't given a sign of life since he said that first sentence. She was still hearing it. 'He's dead.' The words repeated in her head while she sat staring at Giles; face deathly white, blue eyes wide and dark and fixed, like the eyes of a china doll, not the eyes of a living girl. He's dead. He's dead. He is dead, the words crashed and beat inside her, but she didn't believe them, she couldn't bear to believe them.

'They rang me from Zurich,' Giles said. 'Our clients out there heard the news first, and got in touch with me, a couple of hours ago.'

Her eyes flickered then; a deadlier pallor creeping into her face. Malcolm had been dead for hours. While she had laughed and talked, and tried on her wedding dress, Malcolm had been dead in the cold white snow, and she hadn't known.

'I had to break it to my mother first,' Giles said, and there was the faintest note of apology in his voice, or recognition of her claim to have heard sooner. His mouth twisted with a sort of bitterness. 'She took it badly, of course. He was always her favourite. We had to get her a doctor. He gave her a sedative; she's sleeping now.'

Leonie wasn't listening. Her eyes had a fixed, strained look. 'No,' she said suddenly. 'It can't be true. He's on a business trip. He didn't go skiing. You're lying to me. You and your family...you hate me...you've always hated me...' Her voice rose hysterically and she got up, pushing Giles out of the way so angrily that it was like a blow. 'You're lying; I don't believe he's dead!'

Giles grabbed her and she struggled wildly. 'Let go of me! Don't you touch me!'

'Be still, then,' he said through his teeth. 'You're acting crazily. You have to believe it; it's the truth, Leonie. I wouldn't lie about something like this; you know it's true...don't try to pretend it isn't, you'll just go mad.'

She swayed, her eyes closing, and let him push her back on to the chair.

'He shouldn't have been on the ski slopes,' Giles said. He crouched down in front of her and took both her icy hands. He rubbed them slowly, methodically, sending a little wave of warmth through the frozen fingers.

She didn't try to pull them away, because she wasn't really aware what he was doing. She was trying not to believe what he was saying to her. Malcolm couldn't be dead...ten minutes ago she had been looking forward to her wedding, life had been crammed with promise, she had been so happy—and now...

The words echoed in her head again. He is dead. He is dead. She couldn't bear to believe it. If it was true her whole life was over, she was looking into an abyss, into nothing, for ever and ever.

'He should have been in Zurich, but he went off skiing for the weekend, cancelling two business meetings, important ones. Utterly typical,' Giles said curtly. 'He was always going off like that, forgetting the work, just off looking for some fun...'

She got angry then and pushed him away, shaking her head. 'No! Shut up. Don't talk about him! You hated him, too; you hated both of us.' She struggled to her feet again, although he tried to stop her. 'Get your hands off me! Don't touch me!' she muttered thickly, sounding almost drunk.

'You're in shock,' Giles said roughly.

'Leave me alone!' She tried to walk away and fell over the long, flowing skirts of the dress, angrily tearing at it. 'I have to get this off...got to get it off...!' She couldn't bear to wear it, she couldn't bear to feel it against her skin. Her mind brought back the memory of her reflection in the mirror a little while ago. A smiling bride; all white lace and satin. 'Must get it off!' she groaned, straining to reach the zip, and Giles came up behind her. She felt the brush of his cool fingers on her skin and shivered. Then the zip slid down and the dress fell apart, leaving her smooth, pale back bare.

She let the dress slip to the floor and stepped out of it, wearing nothing but a lacy white bra and panties. It didn't even occur to her that Giles was watching her; she wasn't even aware of him.

Kicking her wedding dress aside, she walked like an automaton towards her bedroom. Giles somehow got there first, although she hadn't seen him pass her. He met her, a dressing-gown in his hands.

'Put this on; you'll catch cold.'

She tried to walk past. 'Leave me alone!'

'Leonie, for God's sake!' he muttered hoarsely, his eyes fixed on her averted face.

'Just go away! I don't want you near me!' she whispered.

His mouth indented, but he didn't leave. He took hold of her as if she were a doll, man-handled her forcibly into the dressing-gown.

She resisted, but Giles got his way, of course. He always did—Malcolm had often said so. Giles had not wanted her in the Kent family, and he was getting his own way there. His brother was dead, and she would never be his sister-in-law.

'I hope you're satisfied,' she said bitterly. 'This is what you wanted, isn't it—to stop him marrying me? And now he won't. You must be very happy.'

'Hate me as much as you like; at least that's a healthy emotion,' he said drily. 'But it won't bring Malcolm back to life if you get sick, so I want you to go and lie down now and try to sleep.'

She didn't answer. What did it matter? Nothing in the world mattered now. Malcolm was dead. Malcolm was dead. Thinking it, re-

peating it, did not make it seem any more possible, any more believable.

He tied the belt of the dressing-gown around
her waist, staring down at her white face. 'Is
there someone I can call? Your mother? Shall I
ring her and ask her to come?'

'I don't want anyone.'

'You shouldn't be alone. You must have
someone with you, to look after you. I can't
stay, or I would, but I must get back to my
mother; she'll need me there when she wakes up.
Let me call your mother—what's her number?'

'I don't want her.'

'A friend, then?' he patiently insisted. 'The
one who was making your dress? Did you say
she was coming back soon? I'll call her, shall I?'

'No. Don't call anyone,' she whispered with
the last of her energy. 'I just want to be alone.'
She couldn't start believing in what he had told
her, start bearing it, accepting it, until he had
gone and she was alone, away from watching
eyes and listening ears. 'Please, go away and
leave me alone.'

'Look...' Giles Kent began quite gently, but
Leonie had had enough. She saw the darkness
opening out in front of her and fell forward
into it.

When she recovered consciousness, she was in
bed, the duvet piled over her, the curtains drawn

and the bedroom dark and silent. For a second she blankly did not remember what had happened, and then she did, and, thinking she was alone, she opened her mouth to let out a primal cry; wordless, a groan of agony.

At that somebody moved in the room. Her head twisted on the pillow, her cry bitten off as she stared. The dark shape of a man stood by the window, outlined by a faint glow from a street-lamp outside. He came towards her, bent to look at her, and she saw it was Giles Kent. He had not gone, he was still here.

'I've rung your mother, she should be here within an hour,' he said quietly. 'I'll stay until she gets here. Is there anything I can get you? Some tea? Milk?'

'No,' she said hoarsely. 'I don't want anything, I don't want anyone... I don't want you here...'

'I understand,' he said in that low voice. 'But you're in shock. You shouldn't be alone. A cup of hot tea would help, you know. Let me make one for you.'

Anything to get rid of him, she thought wildly. 'Yes, yes, I'll have tea, then...'

'Good girl,' he said, almost smiling. 'I won't be a moment...'

He went out, closing the door behind him, and she lay there in the bed, her body still icy cold and shivering in spite of the warmth of the duvet. She was alone now, she could cry, but she couldn't, there were no tears, just a terrible anguish eating away at her.

She closed her eyes and saw Malcolm's face; smiling, that teasing, charming smile which made him so irresistible. He had his family colouring; dark hair, pale eyes, height and a slim figure, but in Malcolm they somehow made a different pattern. He was less daunting than his elder brother, much better looking and more light-hearted; a little spoilt, perhaps, by his mother, as Giles had said, but Leonie could understand her spoiling him—Malcolm must have been an adorable little boy. He had often told her Giles was jealous of him, but he had laughed about it, found it funny, even secretly been pleased about it.

Leonie had always felt that Malcolm wasn't yet fully grown up—his mother's partiality had kept a boyishness in him—but she had been sure he would grow out of that once they were married, when they had children of their own.

Now they never would, she thought with a pang of grief that shook her body physically, and that was when the tears began pouring down her face. Shaking with sobs, she couldn't stop them once they had begun, and when the bedroom door opened she had to roll hurriedly on to her face and hide them from Giles.

She heard him put a cup down on her bedside table, and lay still, stifling her sobs and wrenched breathing in her pillow, hoping he would think she was asleep and go away.

He stood there for a second, watching her and listening, then he said quietly, 'I'll be in your sitting-room if you need me. Drink your tea, Leonie, don't let it get cold.'

When he had gone again she sat up, her sobs silenced now but the tears still running down her face. She had always hoped to make friends with Giles and his mother, and his older sister, Linda, who was married, with two children, and lived in Devon, but they had kept their distance and now that, too, was something that would never happen, although Giles was being kind to her, kinder than he had ever been before.

He must be in a state of shock, too, she thought, wiping a hand over her wet eyes and face. When he first arrived she had felt he was angry, and grief took that form sometimes, especially when it came like a blow, out of the blue, and this had, for both of them, for all of them. They might not have liked her, but she had always known that the Kent family were very close, a real family, full of affection, not like her own family, which was why she had longed to become part of them one day, why she had gone on hoping that they would accept her in the end.

Giles had sent for her mother, and Martha would come, naturally. She always did what she knew the world viewed as 'the right thing'; she would be wearing black. She always had a little black dress for every occasion—black was elegant and sophisticated and suited her. She would be muted and sad, but Leonie knew she would get no comfort, or even understanding, from her mother. She wished Giles had not sent for her.

CHAPTER TWO

Two months later, Leonie was stretched out on a beach in Italy, her head shaded by a striped umbrella, her body gleaming with oil and already beginning to take on a pale tan. Angela sat on a beach mattress beside her, painting her toenails a warm shade of pink and occasionally yawning because they had been up late last night at a disco held in their hotel, and had then been awoken early by the splashing and giggling of children leaping into the hotel swimming-pool.

'I shall need a holiday to recover from this!' Angela moaned, and Leonie gave a wry little smile.

'It was your idea to come here!'

'How was I to know this hotel was a whirlpool of mad activity from dawn until the early hours of the morning? It was a good idea at the time; we both needed to get away, didn't we?'

'Yes.'

'You have enjoyed it, haven't you?' Angela asked with an anxious little frown, and Leonie gave her a sideways look, smiling a reassurance.

'You know I have . . . it's magical . . .'

She stared at the shimmering blue sea, the sky arching above it for what seemed an endless distance, and sighed. Magical was the only word she could think of to describe this landscape, especially in the mornings, when the sea and sky seemed new-born, a miracle of changing colours and echoing vistas. For the first couple of days after they had arrived, she had hardly noticed their beauty; she had just plodded obediently with Angela from hotel to beach and back again, as blind to everything around her as she had been ever since Giles Kent had told her Malcolm was dead. Then, slowly, the loveliness of sea and sky had penetrated the ice which had walled her in for weeks, and her eyes had opened on to a new world.

'A holiday—that's what we need,' Angela had said in the flat one rainy May morning. It had been a Saturday, and neither of them had been working.

Leonie had come to dread weekends; she could face life during the week, when she could keep her mind on her work, surrounded by the buzz of busy colleagues, but when she was alone her mood always darkened, and she couldn't stop her thoughts from wandering.

She hadn't said anything to Angela, but she had not needed to—Angela had guessed, or noticed, and had taken to popping in at weekends to keep her company or talk her into coming out.

That morning, Angela had stood by the window looking out over wet gardens full of bedraggled spring flowers; tulips and wallflowers and white lilac. Opposite stretched a vista of wet London roofs. Leonie had been obsessively doing a jigsaw puzzle at the table; it had two thousand pieces and was fiendishly difficult, if not impossible. She had started it the day after Malcolm was buried and so far she had barely done a quarter of it, although she worked at it lethargically during any spare time she had. It gave her something to do.

'Somewhere sunny and foreign,' Angela had said, turning to watch her.

Leonie had carefully fitted an oddly shaped piece of blue sky into the outer rim of the puzzle, then looked up, staring at the grey sky behind Angela's head, realising for the first time that it was raining, and had been raining for days. 'We don't seem to have seen the sun much lately,' she'd flatly agreed.

'So? Shall we do it?' Angela had challenged. 'Come on. Let's walk round to that travel agent in Wilberforce Street and pick up some brochures. It will be fun just looking at them.'

They hadn't needed brochures. The travel agent had told them that there was a fortnight on offer, beginning two weeks later, at a reduced price because it had been under-booked, in Italy, at a lively resort on the Adriatic coast. When he'd shown them a picture of the hotel, and told them the overall cost, Angela had looked eagerly at her.

'What do you think? Shall we? It's a terrific bargain.'

Leonie had hesitated just for a second, but then she had thought of getting away from everything familiar, everything that reminded her of Malcolm, and she had made up her mind.

'Yes, let's go.'

Now they had been here a week and she was very glad she had come. She couldn't say she was happier, exactly; only that she had begun to believe it was possible to be happy again one day. She had begun to lift her head and look about her and notice the world again, and for that much she was very grateful to Angela.

Smiling, her friend relaxed again, screwed the top back on to her bottle of nail varnish, and lay down beside her, closing her eyes. 'Mmm…this is the life. I could stay here, doing nothing but sunbathe, all year round, couldn't you?'

'I wouldn't go so far as to say that! I've an idea it might get boring after a while.'

'Maybe.' Angela stretched again, but her nature was not suited to idleness, and after five minutes' silence she shifted restlessly, turned on to her side and asked, 'Shall we go on this trip this afternoon to Ravenna, to see the Byzantine church?'

Leonie laughed outright at that. 'If you want to! I would quite like to see it, although I don't know much about Byzantine churches. It will make a change from lying on the beach or looking at the shops.'

'That's what I thought,' Angela admitted, caught her friend's amused grin and grinned back. 'Well, we have done a lot of sunbathing!'

The hotel organised a weekly coach trip to the ancient town of Ravenna, an hour's drive away—it was a popular event. When they went to buy their tickets, the girls were told they were lucky to get the last two available, and the coach was already crowded by the time they arrived. They weren't able to sit next to each other. Angela found herself sitting next to a very chatty lady in her late seventies, and Leonie had to sit down next to a skinny young man in denim shorts and a T-shirt, who had already spent a lot of time staring at her in the hotel restaurant.

Delighted, he made the most of his opportunity to get to know her, telling her in a rush that his name was Adrian, he was a trainee architect, and lived with his parents in Sheffield, before going on to ask her endless questions. Where did she live? Did she live alone or with her family? Was Angela her friend or her sister? Where did she work? Oh, a solicitor's office—how interesting; did she like her job?

Leonie kept her replies short and as uninformative as possible, but then he became more personal, shifting closer to her so that his knee touched hers and she could smell the overpowering scent of his manly aftershave.

'I've been dying to get to know you, Leonie... that's a lovely name; I never met anyone called Leonie before. I expect you realised I've been watching you—you're far and away the prettiest girl in the hotel, in the whole town, come to that... but I suppose you've got a boyfriend?'

Leonie was spared having to answer that one, her throat hurting and her face pale under her light tan, because at that moment to her relief they drove up to San Vitale, the Byzantine cathedral in Ravenna, and everyone started exclaiming and staring out of the windows.

'Oh, we're here!' Adrian said, his attention mercifully distracted. 'I'm longing to see the mosaics here; they're the most famous in the Byzantine world, you know.'

'No, I didn't,' admitted Leonie, and he looked round at her with the eagerness of an expert given a chance to educate.

'Really? Oh, yes; in a lot of Byzantine churches the mosaics were defaced or even destroyed centuries ago, especially in places where the Moslems conquered a city, but here in Ravenna they have been kept in marvellous condition, although they date back to the sixth century, and you'll see amazing portraits of the Emperor Justinian and his wife, Theodora. Have you heard about her? The story is that she was once a prostitute, or at least a highly paid courtesan, before she married the emperor—although I don't know how true that is...but...'

As they got off the coach with everyone else Adrian talked on and on in Leonie's ear, stunning her into silence and making Angela give her an amazed and laughing grin. Leonie hurried to catch up with their party, hoping that once the official guide had taken over Adrian would stop talking, but he shadowed her throughout the visit, giving her his own version of the history of Ravenna, until the irritated guide came over and asked him to be quiet while he was in the cathedral.

Then Adrian did lapse into silence, and a few moments later Leonie managed to slip away while Adrian's attention was fixed on the mosaics.

She wandered out into the dazzling Italian sunshine and decided to look at the local shops to see if she could find a present for her mother.

It might placate Martha if she could find something really special; an elegant sweater or a handsome leather bag, both items for which Italy was famous.

Martha Priestley loved clothes and wore them well. Strangers often took Martha for a woman in her late thirties, but, of course, she was a good ten years older than she looked, although she hated admitting it, which was one reason why she had insisted that, from an early age, Leonie should not call her Mother, or Mummy, but should use her first name. Martha loved it if new acquaintances took them for sisters. She hadn't much wanted a child at all, Leonie had soon realised, but Martha positively hated having a grown-up daughter.

'I was a mere child when I was married,' she always said plaintively. She had, in fact, been eighteen when she was married to Leonie's father, and nineteen when Leonie was born, but somehow she made it sound as if she had been a child in school uniform.

If her audience knew Leonie was her daughter, Martha would add with a wistful sigh, 'And then what did he do but die, leaving me alone in the world, with a baby...'

If the audience was a man, who didn't know she had a child, Leonie suspected that her mother did not mention her. It wasn't necessary, because from an early age Leonie had not lived with her mother. After the death of her father, when she was nine, Leonie had been sent to stay with her father's mother, Granny Priestley, down in Hampshire, and there she had stayed until her grandmother died during Leonie's last year at school.

It had not been an unhappy childhood: Leonie had loved her grandmother and known that she, in turn, was loved and needed by a lonely old woman whose husband and only son were dead. It had, in some ways, been idyllic, living in the country, in a village, near the sea and the forest, with ponies to ride and lots of friends at school.

Leonie didn't bear her mother a grievance; she understood that a child did not fit in with the sort of life Martha Priestley wanted and worked hard to achieve for herself.

Now she had a very smart dress shop, and lived in the flat above. She had a circle of like-minded friends, and several male admirers, although she apparently didn't want to marry again. She had found marriage disappointing, and preferred the endless excitement of court-ship to the routine which succeeded a wedding.

She was a very attractive woman—her hair more or less the same shade as Leonie's, but worn in a fine chignon, drawn back to reveal the exquisite bone-structure of her face. Her eyes were paler than her daughter's: a blue close to grey, cold and slightly hard. She relentlessly dieted, and had a wand-like figure. She wore classic clothes, which never went out of fashion, cost a great deal but lasted for years, and suited her perfectly, her cold English beauty at home in black or good tweeds, in pastel twin sets and pearls or in the elegance of Paris designs from Chanel or Dior.

Leonie had grown up seeing very little of her. Indeed, they had only really got to know each other after Leonie got engaged. That was when Leonie really began to understand her mother, and see her clearly, and she had not much liked what she saw.

Malcolm's family was very rich, had a lovely home and moved in social circles Martha had always longed to join—Leonie's news had made her mother very happy. She had begun to plan the wedding at once: it was going to be the social event of the year, if Martha had anything to do with it, and she spared no expense, insisting on making all the arrangements herself.

Malcolm's death had wrecked all those plans, and Martha had been white when she'd arrived at her daughter's flat that day. White, not with grief, but with rage. Leonie would never forget what she had said. 'I've spent a fortune, and all for nothing . . . will his family help me pay the bills?' And later, in a sudden outburst, 'How could he be so reckless? Skiing, just before the wedding...why did you let him go there alone? You should have gone. It wouldn't have happened if you had been there.'

Remembering the sharp, cold voice, Leonie closed her eyes. Ever since her mother had said it she hadn't been able to help wondering... was it true? If she had insisted on going along with Malcolm would he be alive today?

She felt people watching her, and made herself walk on, looking straight ahead. A second later she saw a man sitting at a table in a street café on the other side of the road; their eyes met, and Leonie stopped dead, trembling.

It couldn't be. She was imagining it. A shiver ran down her spine, in spite of the hot Italian sun. Giles Kent? Here?

He got up and strode over to her, looking more casual than she had ever seen him; his cream trousers and open-necked caramel-coloured shirt elegantly relaxed. Designer holiday wear, Leonie thought wildly. She might have expected it from him. He was always perfectly dressed for every occasion.

'What on earth are you doing in Ravenna?' he demanded sharply, as though suspecting her of following him around.

'I'm on holiday,' she snapped back. 'What are *you* doing here?'

'A business trip,' he said in that curt voice, and she winced, turning pale. It had always been

Malcolm who went on these overseas selling
trips—that had been the major part of his job;
he had been good at talking people into buying
the company's products. He had had such
charm and warmth; people always liked him,
and he could probably have sold anything.

'The new sales manager has just gone down
with flu, so I had to take over some of his
work,' said Giles, and she felt grief pour
through her like smoke through a burning
house.

Malcolm was dead; there was someone else
doing his job now, life had to go on without
him. It hurt. She couldn't stop the tears welling
up in her eyes.

Giles watched her with a frown. Her tears
probably embarrassed him; they were embarrassing her. 'Sorry, sorry,' she whispered, turning as if to run away, but Giles moved too and
she cannoned into him, her face coming up
against his chest. Before she could back, his arm
came round her and held her there, his fingers
briefly closing over the back of her head in a
soothing movement while he murmured word-
lessly.

'Ssh . . .'

She stood there, face buried, wanting to let go
completely and cry out all the misery of the past
weeks, but she wouldn't let herself do that, not
with Giles Kent, of all people.

She pulled herself together and straightened up. 'I'm OK now, thanks,' she muttered, grateful for his kindness, and surprised by it because she knew how hostile he had been from the minute his brother had taken her home. Like his mother, he had never thought she was good enough to marry into his family.

'You don't look it!' Giles brutally told her. 'You should sit down for a while.' He propelled her towards the table at which he had been sitting and drew out a chair. Leonie sat down in the shade of a yellow-striped parasol. He was a very overbearing man, she thought as he sat down opposite. She watched his hard face with some perplexity. Even his kindness had a touch of tyranny.

A waiter arrived. 'Coffee?' asked Giles, and she nodded.

'Yes, thank you.'

When the waiter left there was a fraught little silence; Leonie wished Giles wouldn't watch her like that. There was something so male about that tough face, those hard grey eyes, that it made her conscious of being a woman, and that was not an awareness she wanted any more, especially not from him.

'So, why are you here?' he asked quietly, and huskily she repeated,

'On holiday.'

'In Ravenna?' he queried with lifted eye-brows, because although Ravenna attracted many tourists it was not a holiday town.

'No,' she said. 'We're staying at Rimini, having a seaside holiday; sunbathing and swimming. We came to Ravenna on a coach trip.'

'We?' he questioned sharply.

'I'm with Angela, the friend who made my...' She broke off, biting her lip, suddenly remembering that day he'd come to tell her Malcolm was dead and she'd stood there in her wedding dress, her life torn apart as she'd listened.

Giles watched her, his brows together; she wondered if he was remembering, too. What had he thought when she'd begun acting like a crazy woman? She had tried to forget everything about that day, but seeing him again had triggered off the memories—had she really pulled off her wedding dress and kicked it away?

She had been almost out of her mind, she had not cared then what he thought, but suddenly a hot flush swept up her face. She couldn't meet his eyes. She would never have behaved like that normally, stripping off her clothes in front of Giles Kent, of all men!

'Your wedding dress?' he murmured drily, and she knew he remembered. She was afraid of what he might say next, so she began to stammer disconnected words.

'Yes... that beautiful dress... what a terrible... terrible way to treat... something made with such loving care; Angela took such trouble with it...she must have been upset when she saw what had happened to it.'

Leonie broke off suddenly, remembering how delighted she had been just minutes before—staring happily at her reflection in the mirror. The dress had been pure magic, she had loved it; and then Giles had arrived with his bitter news, and she had feverishly pulled off her lovely dress and left it in a heap on the floor. She had never seen it again. Angela must have taken it away with her when she'd come next morning, but she had not said anything, and Leonie had never been able to ask her about the dress. She had wanted to forget everything that had happened that day.

'I'm sure she understood,' Giles said quietly.

Leonie nodded. 'She's my oldest friend; we were at school together. It was her idea to come to Italy—the weather has been so bad in England lately, nothing but endless rain, and Angela felt she had to get some sun. She loves beach life. I think she would be perfectly contented to lie in the sun all day.'

She was chattering stupidly—she didn't really know what she was saying to him—but he made her nervous; she didn't know what he was thinking as he watched her with that thoughtful gaze. He had always been her enemy, he had been dead set against her marriage to his brother, but he no longer seemed so angrily hostile. Well, why should he be now? She was no threat to him and his family any more.

'What about you?' he asked. 'Do you like beach life? Are you happy, lying in the sun all day?'

'Well, it has been a restful week,' she admitted.

'Even though you're so pale I can see you're getting a tan,' he observed, running his glance down over her face, throat and shoulders, and she turned pink again, hoping he had forgotten all about seeing her half naked.

His grey eyes held mockery. 'Maybe I should take another day off and spend it on the beach, too?' he drawled, watching the confusion in her face.

Was he flirting with her? Leonie found it oddly hard to breathe, and was relieved when the waiter arrived at that moment with their coffees. She managed a smile and a shy, *'Grazie!'* She hadn't known a word of Italian until she came here, but now she was beginning to speak a little of the language, enough to communicate with waiters and shopkeepers.

The waiter smiled, said something polite, which she did not understand, and went away. Leonie felt Giles Kent's wry gaze on her but self-consciously didn't meet his eyes. She picked up the small cup instead and gratefully sipped the black liquid it held. Italian coffees rarely seemed the same twice; sometimes she was given a frothy milky coffee, other times a tiny cup of almost lethally strong coffee arrived, and she was only now beginning to sort out what to order.

'Do you speak Italian?' Giles asked, and she shook her head.

'I've picked up a few words, that's all. Do you?'

'Yes,' he said, and she might have expected it. Malcolm had once said that Giles was good at everything; whether at work or play, he'd said, Giles was so successful that he was terrifying.

Malcolm's secretary had interrupted, grimacing, 'You can say that again! He makes me nervous every time he walks into my office!'

'That's because of your guilty conscience, Joanne!' Malcolm had said. 'You're afraid he'll find out how little work you ever do!'

Everyone had laughed, but Leonie had taken the other girl seriously. She could imagine how unnerving it could be to have Giles Kent suddenly walk into your office.

Giles didn't have Malcolm's looks, or charm, of course. He didn't have Malcolm's light touch, either. He didn't chat cheerfully to people who worked for him, make jokes, talk as if he were one of them.

He wasn't exactly popular with the firm's employees. They respected, even admired him, but they made no secret of the fact that they were afraid of him. They certainly did not grin as soon as they saw him, the way they did when they saw Malcolm.

'Are you in Ravenna to sell paper to a client?' she asked him politely, without caring much, but making conversation.

'No, I'm here for the day, too. Of course, I'm not with a coach party...'

'Of course not,' she said with a faint irony that made him look sharply at her. She could not imagine Giles joining a coach party on a day's outing.

'I'm driving myself,' was all he said, though. 'I flew over, naturally, and then I hired a car so that I could get around without needing to use public transport or hire taxis all the time. I prefer to drive myself. I've always wanted to see Ravenna, and since I was only a couple of hours' drive away I decided to fit a visit into my schedule, and I must say it has been worth it.'

She was grateful for a neutral subject to talk to him about, and eagerly said, 'Yes, the Byzantine mosaics are marvellous, aren't they?'

'Breathtaking,' he agreed, and opened a glossy handbook on the table between them, pointing to a photograph of the mosaic portrait of the Emperor Justinian. 'I've often seen photographs of the mosaics here, but to see them in real life gave them a whole new dimension.'

Leonie bent over the handbook, her pale hair falling forward until it almost touched Giles's hand. 'Did you buy that here? The one I got didn't have such terrific photos in it.'

He bent forward, too, brushing her hair back so that he could see the photograph, too. Leonie's head lifted at once, nervously. She was intensely aware of his touch. His face was only inches away; she saw the grain of his skin, his thick black lashes, his tough cheekbones, the curl of his hard mouth. It was an impressive face from a distance, but close to it was even more so. Malcolm had had charm and lighthearted good looks, but Giles Kent had a strength and unshakeable purpose, which one could read in every line of that face.

'Yes, I bought it here,' he said brusquely, his grey eyes so close that she could see every detail of them, the very pale iris, flecked at the rim with tiny yellow rays, the jet black pupil.

The shock of looking into his eyes froze her; she couldn't say a word, and they sat there staring at each other in a sort of trance, the hot Italian sun pouring down, the busy sounds of the town all around them, yet for that instant neither of them was aware of their surroundings. Leonie didn't know what Giles was thinking, nor what she was thinking herself, but she felt the rapid, wild beat of her pulse in her throat, was deafened by the beat of it in her ears.

What on earth was wrong with her? It must be the sun, she thought, her mouth dry. It was making her dizzy.

It was Angela who broke the spell. She rushed up, crossly chattering as she came.

'Oh, there you are! I've been looking all over the place for you. Why did you vanish like that? You might have said you were going! The last I saw of you, you were with that thin boy, what's-his-name, in the cathedral. I saw him chatting you up, so I thought I'd be tactful and fade away, and then you vanished, and he was on his own. I asked him where you were, and he didn't know, and I couldn't see you anywhere. You scared the life out of me. I thought you might have got lost.'

'No, I——' Leonie began, but Angela cut her short more cheerfully.

'No, you just wandered off in a dream, as usual! I should have known. Oh, well . . . come on, I want to get some shopping done before we have to get on the coach.'

'OK,' Leonie said, finishing her coffee hurriedly.

Only then did Angela give the man sitting opposite Leonie a curious, half-suspicious look.

A second later she recognised him, her eyes opening wide, her jaw dropping.

'Hello,' Giles said with dry amusement.

'You...you're...aren't you...?' stammered Angela, for once almost speechless, and Giles nodded, smiling crookedly.

'That's right. You have a good memory. I'm Giles Kent—and you're Leonie's friend, Angela, aren't you?'

'That's right,' Angela said, giving Leonie a stunned look that still managed to fizz with curiosity. What was going on here? her stare asked. What was he doing here? And why hadn't Leonie told her he was going to turn up?

Giles stood up and drew out a chair, gesturing politely. 'Sit down, have some coffee—I'll call the waiter.'

Leonie stood up in a hurry. 'No, we must go. Thank you for the coffee; enjoy the rest of your trip.'

'Enjoy the rest of your holiday,' he said, staying on his feet.

'Thanks,' she said, not quite meeting his eyes because she was suddenly very self-conscious. She slid a hand through Angela's arm and pulled her away, walking fast and not looking back.

Only when they were out of earshot did Angela demand, 'Well? What on earth is going on? What is he doing here, and how did he know you were in Ravenna?'

Halting in front of a shop window to look at some silk blouses, Leonie said, 'He didn't know. We met by sheer chance.'

'Oh, come off it!' Angela said drily. 'That is too big a coincidence.'

'It's true. He's in Italy on a sales trip and he just happened to come to Ravenna because he's always wanted to see the Byzantine remains here. I remember Malcolm saying that Giles was keen on history and was always going off sight-seeing when he was abroad.' Leonie walked on, deciding the silk blouses were too expensive for her.

'I still think it's a massive coincidence that he turned up here while we were here,' Angela said. 'Maybe he was keeping an eye on you?'

Startled, Leonie did a double-take, frowning at her friend. 'Why on earth should he do that?'

'Well, you were almost his sister-in-law— maybe he feels responsible for you?'

Leonie laughed shortly. 'No chance! He doesn't even like me, and he's very glad I'm not going to be his sister-in-law, believe me!'

Angela made a face. 'A pity you aren't. You could have arranged a blind date for me and him.'

Leonie frowned. 'You must be joking!'

'I think he's very sexy,' insisted Angela.

The sun was beating on the top of Leonie's head like a gong; her ears buzzed and she began to feel strangely cold. She swayed, feeling sweat break out on her forehead, and from a long way off heard Angela exclaim, 'Leonie... You aren't going to faint, are you?'

'No,' Leonie whispered, a strange roaring in her ears, and then the next thing she knew was that she was lying on the ground with people standing all round her, staring down at her. Her bewildered eyes roamed the faces and at last found Angela.

Angela anxiously said, 'You fainted—how do you feel now? You're so pale. Are you OK? We'll get a doctor when I can manage to make someone understand what is wanted.' She looked round the circle of staring, curious Italian faces. 'A doctor? Please, a doctor? Oh, what is that in Italian? Oh, I wish I spoke the language...'

As she spoke, someone pushed through the crowd, which parted, almost melted, instinctively before his arrogant assurance and his rapid, insistent Italian.

Leonie looked up at him dazedly, and gave a gasp of horrified shock as she recognised Giles. What was he doing here? She had imagined he would be well on his way by now. She tried to struggle upright, but before she could move he was beside her, one arm going round her waist, the other suddenly behind her knees, lifting her off her feet as if she were a child.

'Oh,' she broke out, blushing to her hairline. 'Put me down, Giles! I'm perfectly OK.'

'Is that why you fainted?' he enquired curtly. 'My car is parked over there; we'll drive to the nearest doctor and find out what's wrong.'

The crowd watched, beaming, enjoying the drama as Leonie wriggled, shaking her head so that her long blonde hair spilled like molten sunshine over the sleeve of his jacket.

'Good idea,' Angela said cheerfully, moving into his angle of vision and smiling. 'I expect someone in that chemist's shop over there could tell us where to find a doctor's surgery.'

Giles gave a brusque nod. 'Will you go and ask them while I'm putting Leonie into my car?'

'Well, my Italian is non-existent,' Angela said. 'What do I say to them?'

He gave her a brief Italian phrase to say. 'Get them to write the address down, too,' he commanded, and Angela gave a military salute, pulling a wry face.

'Yes, sir!'

He half smiled at the mockery, then began to walk away while Angela hurried off to the chemist.

The crowd watched all of them with evident fascination. It was better than a circus, all this exciting drama; they only wished they knew precisely what was going on between these three foreigners. If only they would start speaking Italian so that everyone could follow what was said.

'There's no need to bother a doctor,' Leonie said huskily, but Giles took no notice, his long strides covering the distance to his parked car in no time.

She looked up at him through her lashes and saw his face from a strange angle; the chiselled planes of his face, the taut jaw, the surprising warmth and passionate potential of that hard mouth. Her heart began beating very fast again, and she felt almost sick. It made her breathless to be this close to him, able to see the graining of his face, the rhythmic beat of a pulse in his throat under that tanned skin, and her own reactions were terrifying the life out of her. How could you feel such a violent physical sensation and yet dislike the man touching you?

He must put her down soon; she couldn't bear being this close to him.

'Giles, please,' she whispered, and he looked down at her pausing beside his car, his dark head arrogantly tilted.

'Giles,' she pleaded, her lower lip trembling at the cool way he stared down at her. 'Please,

put me down; I don't need a doctor, I'm not ill,
I'm fine now. It was just the heat, and I think
the coach trip made me feel rather sick, and
then walking around the cathedral...but I'll be
OK now.'

'You ought to see a doctor!' he merely said.

She was as flushed now as she had been white
when she had first recovered consciousness.
Held in his arms like this, how could she fight
these disturbing responses to his touch, his
nearness?

'Well, I don't want to!' she muttered crossly.
'Stop bullying me! You're always trying to push
me around, and I hate it!'

He lowered her into the front passenger-seat
of his car. 'Then if you won't see a doctor I'll
drive you back to your hotel in Rimini.'

'There's no need for you to go out of your
way! I can go back on the coach with every-
body else.'

He bent down and caught her face in his
hand, pushed it back and stared frowningly
down at her, his eyes glittering like dark stars.

'Why are you so obstinate?'

'Why are you?' she said, deeply aware that he
was staring down at her mouth. She wanted to
scream at him: stop it! Stop looking at me like
that. You don't know what you're doing to me!
But she couldn't say anything, of course, or
even hint that he was having this bewildering

effect on her. It was probably all in her own fevered imagination, this intense awareness of him. He didn't even like her; he never had.

'I'm being sensible; you aren't,' he said curtly. 'Look, I'll drive you back to make sure you don't faint again, and when we get back to the hotel I'm going to insist you see a doctor.'

Leonie didn't bother to argue any more because Angela was running towards them.

'They gave me a list of local doctors,' she panted, holding out a printed sheet which held telephone numbers and addresses. 'I think the nearest one is——'

Giles interrupted. 'Leonie prefers to go back to Rimini and see a doctor there. I'll take her in my car, to save waiting around for this coach to start back.'

'Oh, that's great,' Angela said cheerfully. 'I'll hop into the back, shall I?'

Through her lowered lashes Leonie saw Giles frown, but Angela didn't wait for him to answer; a moment later she was in the back seat of the car and after a brief pause Giles got behind the wheel and switched on the engine.

Leonie leaned back, her eyes closed, hoping Giles wouldn't speak again until they reached Rimini. Angela was rattling on from the back, telling him about their holiday, asking about his work, asking about his mother's health. Giles answered coolly, politely, but Leonie sensed that his mind was on something else. Secretly she watched his hands on the wheel; they moved with such certainty and long-fingered deftness. Giles was a very confident man; she wished she had his certainty about himself and life. Her gaze flicked down sideways to observe the rest of his body; he was strongly built, yet graceful, with that deep chest, slim waist, and long legs. Angela kept talking about how sexy he was; maybe that was why she, herself, couldn't apparently think about anything else?

Her face burned as she suddenly realised that while she had been assessing his body he had been watching her do so.

His brow lifted mockingly. 'Well?' he murmured, his voice so low that only she heard.

Leonie pretended not to have heard, though. Hot-faced, she turned her head away and stared out of the window without answering. She was furious when she heard Giles laugh. What on earth must he be thinking?

She didn't look his way again and stayed silent, but it was an enormous relief to drive up to their Rimini hotel some time later. Giles came round to help her out of the car, and she muttered a hurried thank you, but refused point-blank to see a doctor, in spite of everything Giles said.

'I told you, I fainted because of the heat,' she said firmly. 'I don't want to see some foreign doctor; he probably wouldn't understand a word I said, and I certainly wouldn't understand him, so just forget it, will you?'

'Well, at least promise me that if you feel ill again you'll get a doctor at once!' he said impatiently, and she promised, her fingers crossed behind her back.

'I'd better be on my way,' Giles said.

'Oh, stay for dinner!' invited Angela eagerly, but after a brief glance at Leonie's shuttered and averted face Giles coldly said he couldn't stay any longer, he had to get up early in the morning.

'Thank you very much for your help,' Leonie said rather distantly, knowing that Angela was pulling faces at her behind his back, silently ordering her to plead with him not to go yet.

He nodded, his mouth wry and crooked, then he had gone, and Angela burst out crossly, 'Why were you so offhand with him? If you'd asked him I'm sure he would have stayed for dinner!'

'I didn't want him to. I'm going to bed early!'

'You may be!' Angela said, her eyes accusing. 'I'm not! I may never get another chance to seduce him!'

'Sorry about that!' Leonie said insincerely, walking away towards the lift. 'But I'm going to bed now.'

It wasn't until she was back in England that she went to see a doctor, and then the suspicion that had begun to grow in her mind was finally confirmed.

She was pregnant.

CHAPTER THREE

'OH, LEONIE! What on earth are you going to do?' Angela said, looking aghast.

'Have it,' Leonie said, her face obstinate.

'But have you thought...? It will be so difficult, bringing up a baby alone!'

'Yes, of course I know that, but I'll manage, somehow. It will be worth it, to have Malcolm's baby!'

Angela blew her nose and looked fierce, then said, 'Do you think they'll let you go on working in your office until you have the baby?'

'I hope so,' Leonie said, but her voice was not confident. The head of the legal firm she worked for was a very old-fashioned man in his late sixties, and she suspected he would be taken aback when he discovered that she was going to have a child.

'Well, they can't sack you for it!' Angela said belligerently. 'Not in this day and age!'

Leonie wasn't too sure about that, her blue eyes rueful because she had already been over this argument, mentally, with herself, and she couldn't decide what might happen when her boss found out. 'For the moment, I'm not telling anyone at the firm,' she admitted. 'Mr Rawlings is as blind as a bat, and the others may not notice for a while, so I should have time to look about for another job.' She sighed. 'And somewhere to live.'

Angela was frowning. 'Won't you be able to stay on in this flat? They can't turn you out because you've had a baby! That's inhuman. There is plenty of room here.'

'Yes, but in my tenancy agreement it says that I cannot have pets or children in the flat—these flats are meant for single people; that's why they're so tiny.'

Angela bit her lip. 'Oh. But is it binding? I mean, you could fight them . . .'

'I'd lose. I haven't worked for a solicitor for years without finding out quite a bit about the law, and I signed that agreement, knowing what it meant.'

'But what will you do? I wish I could help, but you know there simply wouldn't be room for anyone else in my flat.' Angela's was a studio flat; one very spacious room which served her as bedroom, kitchen and sitting-room, and in which she also worked at her dressmaking, plus a tiny bathroom.

'Of course there wouldn't, although it's nice of you even to think about it!' Leonie said, smiling at her friend gratefully. 'Oh, don't worry, I'll find somewhere, Angela. I'm a good secretary, I'll get good references from Mr Rawlings if he does want me to leave my job—and, you know, even if he says I can stay on, I may have to go because London rents are so high. I doubt if I could afford them if I had a baby to keep, too. I'll have to find someone to look after the baby while I work, and that will cost money, so I may have to leave London.'

'Leave London?' Angela sounded absolutely horrified. A Londoner born and bred, she couldn't imagine living anywhere else, and her expression was that of someone hearing that a friend had been condemned to exile from everything safe and beloved. 'But you won't know anyone—all your friends are in London! I think it would be a mistake to move to a strange place just when you're going to need support, Leonie. Don't even think of it.' Angela broke off. 'Unless . . . do you mean you're going to live with your mother?'

Leonie gave her a wry look, shaking her head. 'That wouldn't please my mother! She isn't really family-orientated, you know. She never wanted me when I was a child; she won't want me around now that I have a baby of my own.'

'Does she know?' Angela watched pink colour creep up Leonie's face and her blue eyes darken.

'Not yet. I'm waiting for the right moment to break it to her.' Leonie gave her a rueful look. 'If I told her now she would try to browbeat me into getting rid of the baby while it is still possible, and I don't want that, so I won't tell her until I have to.'

Nodding, Angela vaguely murmured, 'Probably wise...' Then she said with hesitation, 'What about Malcolm's family? Couldn't they help? After all, this is his baby, and if he was alive it would be his responsibility, and the Kents are a rich family—they could easily afford to help you...'

'No!' Leonie said, turning dark red, her voice shaking with anger and determination.

Angela stared, looking amazed. 'But why not? Surely... after all, it will be Mrs Kent's grandchild!'

'No, I don't even want them to know about it!'

'You can't be serious!' gasped Angela. 'You don't even mean to tell them you're having Malcolm's baby?'

'No.' Leonie pushed back her fine silvery hair, leaving her delicate profile exposed, and for the first time Angela could see a resemblance between her and her mother. Leonie's face might have a fragile bone-structure, but it was set, determined, and it had a strength Angela had never noticed in it before.

'But why not?' Angela couldn't understand Leonie's attitude at all.

Leonie's blue eyes glittered with hostility. 'They didn't want me in their family. They didn't even answer the invitations to the wedding; they probably wouldn't have come. Oh, Giles Kent has been quite kind to me since...' Her voice quivered and she bit down on her lower lip, then took a deep breath and went on, 'Since Malcolm died... When he came to tell me, that day, he was a bit brutal at first, but when he saw I was knocked sideways by it he started being quite kind, and then in Italy, when I walked into him in the street, he was almost nice...'

'He's certainly sexy,' said Angela, grinning. 'I wouldn't say no to a date with Giles Kent!'

Leonie gave her a startled frown. 'You must be crazy! Sexy is the last word I'd apply to Giles Kent!'

'It isn't me that's crazy! It's you. And blind, too! He's got all that power and money... they're potent aphrodisiacs, for a start!'

'Well, you're welcome to him,' Leonie said flatly. 'But I don't want anything to do with him, or any of them.'

'But they have lots of money——'

'That's why I'm not telling them! They might try to take the baby away from me.'

'They couldn't do that!'

'I think they might—after all, they could obviously give the baby a luxurious home, whereas I'm going to have a hard struggle to manage...'

'But isn't that exactly why you are going to need their help? I'm sure they wouldn't try to take the baby away—but they might give you an allowance which would make all the difference!'

'I don't want their money.'

'Oh, but Leonie...'

Face stubborn, Leonie said, 'Please, Angela, drop the subject! I've made up my mind about this. I am not going to tell the Kent family anything, and don't you tell anyone, either. Promise.'

Angela reluctantly promised. Sighing, she asked, 'So, if you aren't going to live with your mother, where are you going to live?'

They spent the next hour discussing possibilities: trying to think of some part of the country where Leonie could get a job, find someone to look after the baby while she worked, but still afford to rent a flat. It was a dispiriting and fruitless discussion.

A month later Leonie began to notice people giving her a second look, their eyes startled and disbelieving at first. She went a little pink, and waited for a comment, but perhaps nobody liked to say anything, since she had not dropped any hints and they weren't sure they were not imagining things. Then people started standing in huddles, whispering, until she appeared, when they would hurriedly spring apart and disappear in all directions without meeting her eyes.

After a few days of this, her boss gruffly asked her to come into his office one morning, and, after clearing his throat a few times and fiddling with the papers on his desk, muttered, 'Miss Priestley, I am sorry to have to ask you this, it is very embarrassing for both of us, but...there is some gossip in the office... I am told that people think...that...'

Leonie was sorry for him, he was finding it so hard to get the question out, so she answered it without his needing to ask.

'Yes, I am going to have a baby, Mr Rawlings,' she said quietly.

He let out a long sigh. 'Oh, dear. I...I am very sorry to hear that...'

'I am not sorry to be having it, Mr Rawlings,' Leonie said at once, her voice husky. 'I was happy when I knew; it will be some compensation for losing Malcolm, to have his child.'

Mr Rawlings picked up a pencil and doodled on a sheet of paper without looking at her. 'I have every sympathy, of course, and we are not so behind the times that we take a moral attitude, I assure you . . . but how will you manage to go on working after the child arrives?'

'If I can find someone to take care of it until I get home each evening . . .' she began, and he looked at her at last, kindly, with pity.

'You couldn't possibly afford a full-time nanny on your salary, Miss Priestley. My daughter has a baby and still works, but quite a sizeable chunk of what she earns goes to pay the nanny. If she weren't married she would never be able to manage. I think you aren't being very realistic. But, if you can make some arrangement of the sort, of course you can keep your job, and we will allow you the usual maternity leave. I will get an agency secretary in until you can come back, but please let me know well in advance whether or not you will definitely be coming back. If you are not able to make some arrangement for the child to be cared for full-time, you can always carry on working here in another capacity, perhaps part-time, or work flexible hours to enable you to spend time with your baby.'

She was grateful that he was allowing her to stay on in her job until the birth; that gave her a useful breathing-space. At least he wasn't telling her to go at once. She had suspected he might. His office was highly respectable and dealt with some very wealthy, often quite elderly, and at times narrow-minded clients. This might be the end of the twentieth century, but she often thought that some of their clients were not aware of that fact.

'Thank you, Mr Rawlings; I promise to let you know, well in advance, what arrangements I've been able to make,' she said.

She was just as fortunate in the agents who represented the owner of her flat. They at once pointed out that she could not be permitted to have a baby living in the flat, but agreed with some sympathy that she could stay on until after the birth, so she had a breathing-space during which she was sure she would come up with something.

She started hunting for another flat at once, but London prices were so high, and landlords tended not to want unmarried mothers as tenants unless they could afford massive rents. She still had two and a half months before the birth, but time was passing so quickly.

The last person to find out that she was going to have a baby was the one she might have told first if her mother had been different. Leonie had not seen her since her angry, resentful reaction to Malcolm's death, but, when Leonie was a little more than six months pregnant, her mother arrived at the flat one Saturday afternoon without warning.

Leonie opened the door and her mother froze on the spot, staring fixedly, her cold eyes opening wide in shock.

'You had better come in,' Leonie said wearily, holding the door and standing to one side to let her pass.

Her mother walked into the flat, Leonie closed the door and followed her into the sitting-room, waiting for the storm to break over her head.

Swinging to face Leonie, Martha let her pale blue eyes flick down over her, her nostrils flaring in anger and distaste. 'When is it due?' she asked, and, when Leonie had answered that, at once asked icily, 'It is Malcolm Kent's, I presume?'

Hot coins of red in her face, Leonie snapped back, 'Yes, it is!'

Martha's lips thinned. 'I thought you had more brains than to let this happen to you! I can see why you stayed away and never said a word to me about it! Well, at least his family can afford to support you, that is one mercy!'

Leonie looked aside, biting the inside of her lip.

Martha's eyes narrowed and she sharply asked, 'They are going to help you, aren't they?'

Leonie took a long breath. 'I don't want to involve them—— '

'Don't be ridiculous!' Martha interrupted. 'What did they say when you told them? Didn't they offer to——?'

'I didn't!' Leonie said shortly.

'What?' Martha was red with anger now. 'Are you telling me that they don't know? You stupid girl! Of course you must tell them. They have plenty of money, and you have a right to some of it. I'll speak to them if you're so proud that you can't bring yourself to!'

'Don't you dare!' Leonie desperately burst out, for once having the courage to contradict her mother to her face.

Martha Priestley looked disbelievingly at her, stiffening, and for once wordless. 'Stay out of it,' Leonie went on less fiercely. 'I want nothing more to do with Malcolm's family. They hate me; they didn't want me when Malcolm was alive, and I'm not going begging to them. I would rather live on welfare than ask them for a penny.'

She hadn't silenced her mother, of course. Martha was shaking with rage, and she had a lot to say, firing the words at her daughter like bullets.

'You can't afford to be so high-minded! And neither can I! You know very well I wanted to ask the Kent family to help me pay the bills I was left with for that wedding. Some things could be cancelled—the reception and the church, the wedding cars, the flowers... but a lot of things still had to be paid for. The invitations, the cake, that real lace veil you were going to wear...the accessories, your white shoes, your trousseau ... oh, I know it was my present to you, but the bill was enormous! And then there was my own dress...'

She caught Leonie's eye and flushed angrily, although her daughter hadn't said a word. 'Well,' Martha defended herself sharply, 'I had to have something special; I didn't want the Kents to think their son was marrying into a poor family. I had a dress made by a famous designer, and I couldn't hand it back, I had to pay for it—I would never have bought anything so expensive for myself; I only ordered it for your wedding. I have always been very careful with money, and, let me tell you, I hated running up debts of that sort, and I couldn't see why the Kents, with all their wealth, should not have been asked to help. After all, it would have been their son's wedding as much as yours, and I was extravagant only because I wanted to make sure the wedding was a grand affair, an occasion to which all the Kent family and friends could come with pride.'

'I know,' Leonie said unhappily, wishing she would stop talking about it. Her own anxieties over her pregnancy had somehow eased her pain over Malcolm's death; it wasn't that she had forgotten him or that she missed him less—indeed, she often thought of him when she thought of her baby—but she had so many other problems on her mind, and time kept ticking by like a racing clock. In a few months now she would be having her baby, and she needed to get her life sorted out first.

'I don't think you do!' Martha snapped at her. 'I did not, in fact, ask the Kents for help, in the end, because you became almost frantic when I spoke to you about it. But that meant that I was left to bear the burden of that debt, when in my opinion the Kents might have offered to help me! And if you think that I am going to help you carry the cost of Malcolm Kent's baby, you are very much mistaken!'

'I didn't ask you to help!' Leonie said, on the point of tears. 'I'm sorry if you got into debt on my behalf; I wish I had the money to pay you back now, and one day when I do have some money I will pay you, but I'm not asking you for money now, or for help, or... or anything... I'll manage, somehow.'

Martha stared at her, breathing hard, her cold blue eyes like marble, her fine-boned face clenched in fury. Leonie flinched, afraid of what she might be going to say, but her mother simply walked past her and slammed out of the flat.

On a Saturday Leonie did the shopping and the housework, so she was able to push the thought of her mother to the back of her head while she concentrated on her usual weekend routine. She found it rather more tiring at the moment, of course, so she didn't try to rush about, but took it slowly and easily.

She ate a light salad lunch once her work was finished, and then lay down for an hour, but she had no sooner closed her eyes than the doorbell rang, and she sighed and trudged back up the corridor.

She expected Angela, who often dropped in on a Saturday afternoon for a chat or a cup of tea, but when Leonie opened the front door she was appalled to find herself looking into the cold grey eyes of Giles Kent.

She couldn't get a word out, flinching in alarm, waiting for his first reaction to the sight of her, but as she stared at him she realised that he already knew she was pregnant. His face didn't register shock or incredulity; he ran one brief glance over her heavy body and then he took a step forward, into the flat, forcing her to step back out of his way.

Leonie's mind was racing. He had known before she'd opened the door. Someone had told him! My mother! she thought bleakly. It has to be my mother; she was the only one who would have done it. In spite of everything I said to her—oh, how could she?

And *what* did she say to him exactly? What did she ask him to do? Leonie's hands screwed up into tight little balls of tension and misery. Martha had asked for money, for some financial arrangement, of course—that was why she did it. Money has always been what mattered most to her. I told her I didn't want anything from the Kents; I told her exactly how I felt... how could she?

'You're not looking well,' Giles said abruptly, and she gave him an incredulous look.

'You may not have noticed, but——'

'You're pregnant, I know; I am quite observant enough to notice that, I assure you,' he said with a dry intonation. 'But I've always understood that pregnant women looked radiantly healthy, and you are very pale and listless. Are you taking care of yourself?'

'Yes, thank you,' she said in a mock-submissive voice, and he half smiled, a quick crook of the mouth before his lips straightened again.

'Sit down,' he ordered in that peremptory way of his, gesturing to a chair, and Leonie, with a sigh of resignation, obeyed, saving her energy for whatever argument might be going to follow. She was determined not to let the Kent family interfere in her life, but she suspected Giles was not going to give in easily.

Once she was seated, Giles sat down, too, near by, leaning forward, his black hair lit with a halo of the autumnal sunlight filtering down behind him, through a plane tree in the street outside. His face was half in shadow as he stared at her; she couldn't guess what he thought about her situation, but then Giles Kent could, when he chose, always hide what he was thinking.

'Your mother rang me,' Giles told her without a flicker of expression, and a wave of hot colour swept up Leonie's face.

Angrily, she burst out, 'I suspected she had when I saw you outside, but she did that without my permission. I told her not to get in touch with your family!'

'I know, she mentioned that,' Giles said, with dry irony. 'It was a very frank conversation.'

Leonie winced, embarrassment in her eyes as she looked down. 'If she asked you for money, please forget it——'

'She didn't ask me for money,' he interrupted curtly. 'Well, not directly. Of course, she did point out how difficult life was going to be for you when you had the baby. She explained that she wanted to help you, but she had financial problems of her own at the moment. She explained that there was a large debt she had incurred because the wedding had had to be cancelled.'

'Oh, no!' Leonie said, biting her lower lip. She looked up then, her darkened lashes flicking against her pale cheek. 'I'm sorry...'

'Why should you be?' Giles coolly returned. 'I blame myself for letting her get into debt. It should have occurred to me long ago that there might be a financial problem. I imagined Malcolm would have seen to it that the wedding expenses were not left to your mother to pay—she is a widow living on a small income, and I can see it must be difficult for her. I'll deal with her problem immediately. I only wish I had thought of it before, but...' He paused, frowning, his mouth incisive. 'But I had other things on my mind, I'm afraid.'

Leonie watched him, her dark blue eyes sensitive to the tension in his face. She could guess what he was thinking about. Her own grief at the loss of Malcolm was mirrored in the Kent family; she had not forgotten how Malcolm's mother must have felt these past months and she had often regretted that the dislike Mrs Kent felt towards her meant she was unable to give her the comfort and support she must have needed.

'How is your mother?' she asked gently, and Giles looked up, his gaze flicking across the room to her again.

'She has been in a state of deep depression for months.'

'I'm sorry,' Leonie murmured.

He nodded. 'From the look of you, so have you!'

She didn't answer that, and he went on, 'She is finding it hard to come to terms with Malcolm's death; he was always her favourite child—I suppose mothers always feel a soft spot for their youngest, and Malcolm had a lot of charm. It hit her very hard, and she won't accept professional help, she won't see a therapist or even talk about her feelings, which might help. Bottling it all up inside herself just makes the situation worse, her grief is feeding on itself—I've become increasingly worried about her.'

'I can quite understand why she doesn't want to see a psychiatrist, or talk about it,' Leonie thought aloud with sympathy. Mrs Kent was a woman of great pride; she would hate the idea of confiding her innermost feelings to anyone, especially to a stranger, and Leonie imagined that she would equally dislike the idea of having analysis. She would probably think that it was shameful, and would be afraid of her friends finding out, of being talked about, even laughed at.

'You and my mother have more in common than she realises,' Giles said, staring narrow-eyed at her, and she flushed, her look startled. Before she had time to think about that remark, Giles went on, 'I have been at my wits' end, trying to think of a way to get through to her; nothing I could do seemed to help. When your mother rang me today it was like a gift from heaven—I realised at once what it would mean. This is going to snap my mother out of her depression; this baby is going to give her something to live for. It will be like giving Malcolm back to her. So you don't need to worry any more, or agonise about ways and means of coping on your own, Leonie. From now on, you can leave everything to us.'

CHAPTER FOUR

THAT was what Leonie had been afraid of, what she had dreaded, and she burst out anxiously, angrily, 'No! I don't care what my mother told you, she wasn't talking for me. I may have problems, but they are my own business, nobody else's, and I can deal with them. This baby is mine, and I want it, I'm keeping it—I can take care of it myself without any help from my mother, or you, or anybody. I'm certainly not giving it up.'

Giles's eyes narrowed and hardened, and she reacted instinctively to the threat of his stare, in a flare of fear, her dark blue eyes wide and strained, stumbling to her feet with the ungainly movement of a pregnant woman, her body heavier than she ever remembered until she tried to move fast.

'Be careful!' Giles said roughly, and suddenly there he was, next to her, his arm around her, supporting her. 'You shouldn't have got up so suddenly! You have to take care of yourself now, for the baby's sake.'

'I'm OK, thank you!' she muttered, stiffening as she became aware of the warmth of his skin, the firmness of bone and muscle under that. His hands pressed into her back, his fingers splayed, each pressing down into her own flesh.

It was a long time since she had been in anyone's arms, held close; the human contact was tempting, the comfort one she often longed for in the dark hours of the night when she was alone and aching with loneliness and need. She tried to be strong and brave, but sometimes she broke down. It was only human to need to be held, to be close to another living body—but she mustn't give in to that need, let him go on holding her and stroking that warm hand up and down her back.

It might become a habit; she might come to need it, need him. After all, this wasn't even the first time she had broken down and he had been there to help her. It disturbed her to remember that when they met in Ravenna she had cried in his arms, and now she was close to doing so again, the tears only just held back. It wasn't wise; after all, he might seem gentle and kindly now, but she mustn't forget the cold hostility he had shown her right up until his brother had died.

He had only become kinder because she was no longer any threat to himself or his family—

so what did that tell her about him? Giles Kent was a man whose head ruled his life. He coolly decided how to deal with everyone around him, for reasons which had nothing to do with his emotions—if he had any emotions they were never allowed to show, or to influence how he behaved. It would be folly to forget that, especially now that everything had changed again.

'You don't look very OK to me,' Giles said drily, his mouth moving close to her hair, stirring the delicate silvery strands with his breath. 'You may not want our help, Leonie, but it's obvious you need it.'

She had something he wanted; she was carrying his brother's child, the baby he felt might make his mother happy again—and Giles wanted it. Malcolm had often said with a mixture of wry admiration and faint resentment that Giles was relentless in pursuit of what he wanted; he had a powerful will, a tenacity of purpose. That was what made him so good at running the family business, Malcolm had said, grimacing as though he'd wished he were cut from the same stuff. Malcolm had been a warm, lovable human being, though, not a man of iron.

No, Giles was not made of iron; his metal was altogether more invulnerable—that was what made him such a dangerous enemy to make. You couldn't get through his defences, he was impervious, and he was always determined to have his own way. Leonie knew that if she refused to do what he wanted he would stop smiling at her, being gentle and protective—she would see his icy enmity show through again.

But she wasn't afraid of Giles—she had too much to lose if she weakened—so she pulled away and faced him defiantly, her chin up. 'I *can* take care of myself—and the baby, too! I've always taken care of myself, since I left school, and I'll manage somehow, now that there will be two of us. My mother managed to bring me up all on her own.' Her eyes moved away from his face, and she frowned, remembering her childhood, her own bewilderment and loneliness. Well, she wouldn't send her baby away, whatever happened, however hard it might be to keep it. At all costs, she wouldn't repeat the mistakes her mother had made. Somehow, she would manage to keep her baby with her.

His eyes were bitingly ironic, his voice brusque. 'Do you really want your baby to grow up the way you did?'

She drew a startled breath, looking up into his eyes. She had never confided in him, ever told him anything about her lonely childhood. How did he know all about that? Malcolm? Or had he had her background investigated as soon as he'd discovered that his brother meant to marry her?

'I'll make sure my baby is happy,' she said firmly, lifting her chin, defiance in her blue eyes.

'You'll have to go out to work, and that means you won't be with the baby very much, you know that,' Giles said, his black brows heavy.

'I've thought it all out,' she insisted. 'Plenty of other women manage, and so shall I. As long as my baby knows I love it, and want it, everything will work out in the end.'

His hard mouth parted impatiently, to snap out some disbelieving reply, but she spoke first, angrily.

'Look, this baby is my problem, and I'll solve it somehow; I'll manage. I'm sure you only mean to be kind, but I'd really rather you didn't.' Before he could go on arguing, she rushed on, 'I'm sorry about your mother. I would have been to see her before if I had thought she wanted to see me—it would have helped me to talk to her, you know. After all, we're both grieving for Malcolm, we both miss him badly. But I knew she wouldn't want to see me; I suppose I would have reminded her that she and Malcolm had been arguing for weeks before he was killed. It must be hard for her to remember that, but I'm sure Malcolm wouldn't want her to blame herself, I'm sure he has forgiven her. And . . . well, if she wants to see the baby when it has been born, she'll be very welcome to come and see us any time she likes, or I'll bring the baby to visit her, but only if it is understood that my baby stays with me.'

Giles had decided to change his tactics now. Instead of being domineering and trying to force her to do as he demanded, he tried a soothing voice, a smile that held some of Malcolm's charm.

'Of course it will!' he assured her, pretending to look surprised. 'You didn't think I wanted to take it away from you, did you? Of course I don't. I wouldn't dream of it.'

She wasn't convinced, though. How could she trust him, knowing the ways in which he and his mother had tried to stop her marrying Malcolm?

'Well, I'm glad about that,' she said, the defiance still glittering in her blue eyes. 'As long as you understand how I feel about everything.'

There was an impatient, obstinate look about him, and she didn't want him arguing any more so she gave a deliberate yawn. 'I don't want to be rude, but I was just going to take a nap when you arrived . . . so if you don't mind . . . ?'

He gave her a searching look and nodded. 'Yes, you look pretty drained. Anxiety is no good for a woman in your condition, Leonie . . . you don't need all that tension . . .'

'It isn't an illness, you know! I'm going through a perfectly healthy, natural process; it hasn't turned me into a helpless invalid,' she muttered, walking to the front door and pointedly opening it.

He took the hint, shrugging, but paused before leaving and studied her flushed face. 'Malcolm would want us to do what we can to take care of you,' he said, and that really was below the belt. She gave him a furious look.

'I don't remember you being so concerned about Malcolm's feelings when he was alive!'

His jawline tightened and he frowned blackly. 'Maybe I've learnt a lot since the day my brother died,' he said in a low, harsh voice, and then he walked away and Leonie bit her lip, staring after him and feeling ashamed and guilty.

When she talked to Angela later, she wasn't surprised by her friend's reaction—Angela made it quite clear that she thought she was mad, and ought to accept whatever the Kent family wanted to give her.

'After all, the baby will be one of their family,' said Angela forcefully, 'Even though you and Malcolm hadn't got around to marrying yet. You would have done if Malcolm hadn't been killed, so you're entitled to a claim on the Kents. You know very well it is going to be tough, bringing up a baby without any help from anyone. You haven't got anywhere to live after the baby is born, you may not even have a job...what are you going to do if you turn down the offer Giles Kent made you?'

'I don't know,' Leonie said wearily. 'Don't bully me, Angela. I got enough of that from Giles Kent.'

'You mean you know I'm making sense!' Angela said drily, but she didn't go on trying to convince Leonie; she merely shrugged and started to talk about her new boyfriend, Andrew.

Her last one, Jack, had recently been transferred by his firm to another part of the country. He had suggested that they kept in touch, wrote, saw each other whenever possible, but Angela had shaken her head. She was far too practical not to see the pitfalls ahead. 'It would never work,' she had said to him bluntly. 'I couldn't bear to live anywhere but London, and I couldn't afford to travel back and forth to see you all the time. It would soon drive us both mad. Better to split up now, and stay friends. If you're ever in London, give me a ring, but if you find someone else, date her with my blessing, because, frankly, I shall do the same.'

Angela was very independent; she had her life worked out and running smoothly, she could take care of herself and was ambitious for the future. Although she loved men's company, she had never yet felt she could not live without any one of them, but there was something new in the way she talked about her latest boyfriend, a young doctor at a London teaching hospital. Leonie wasn't sure what was different—a touch of breathlessness? A flush on her cheeks? A brightness in the eyes?

'When am I going to meet Andrew?' Leonie asked her curiously, and Angela promised to give a little supper party in her flat one evening soon.

'You'll like Andrew,' she assured her, adding, 'We'll just have a few people. There isn't room for more than a dozen. Something simple to cook and serve ... a paella, or pasta ... they can help themselves in the kitchen and then sit down on the floor to eat. Some garlic bread! Fruit ... and wine ... Perfect.'

'Can I opt out of sitting on the floor to eat?' Leonie wryly asked. 'I may get down there, but I'm not sure I shall be able to get back up again!'

Angela looked down at her heavy body and laughed. 'Sorry, stupid of me! Of course you can sit on a chair.'

She continued to plan aloud, 'I'll ask people to bring a bottle of something, too. Whatever they can afford, preferably wine.'

'I'll help you with the food,' offered Leonie, glad to have something to keep her mind off her own problems.

It wasn't as if she could do much about them as yet. She still had nine weeks to go before the baby arrived, she was sure she would find somewhere to live before then, and the local health clinic had given her the names of several women who might agree to take care of the baby while she went on working. Leonie had met two of them and liked them, but until the baby had actually arrived she felt she couldn't make any firm arrangements. She would get six weeks' leave after the birth, which meant that she wouldn't have to make a final decision for over three months.

In one way that was a relief, but in another the uncertainty was worrying and unsettling. She didn't know what the future held, she didn't know if she could cope, and her pregnancy meant that she was often tired—her life was a mess.

Angela's party was something to look forward to, and she enjoyed helping her get ready for it. They cooked a huge paella, which they then covered with silver foil and kept hot in a low oven, they prepared bowls of salad, and Leonie made an enormous chocolate mousse, which was popped into the fridge an hour before the guests arrived.

Angela had bought a few bottles of red and white wine to start the party off, and was hoping everyone would bring a bottle too, to keep things going with a swing.

The first to arrive was Andrew, and Angela greeted him with flushed excitement, especially when she saw what he was carrying under each arm—two bottles of champagne!

'Very extravagant of you, but marvellous! You're a love!' she said, throwing her arms around his neck and kissing him.

Leonie liked him on sight; he was tall and skinny with dark brown hair and hazel eyes, not good-looking exactly, but with such a warm smile that nobody could help smiling back.

'This is Leonie,' Angela said casually, waving a hand at her. 'You remember, I told you about her?'

Leonie flushed—what had Angela told him? She didn't much like the thought that Angela had been gossiping about her to someone she hadn't even met.

She met his hazel eyes uncertainly, and Andrew gave her a friendly grin, offering his hand. 'Hi, I'm Andrew, and judging from your wary expression you're doing just what I'm doing—wishing you knew just what she has been saying!'

Leonie laughed, relaxing. 'Something like that!'

'Oh, don't be so silly, the pair of you,' said Angela. 'There's the doorbell again—I'll go and open the door while you open the champagne, Andrew. Leonie, find some suitable glasses!'

'She loves to give orders, doesn't she?' Andrew teasingly asked, but Angela just rushed off to let in the new arrivals, who were also carrying bottles, to Angela's delight and relief.

The room was soon crowded with people and humming with voices, and it was several hours before Leonie ran into Andrew again. She was carrying a tray of clean glasses from the kitchenette, where she had just washed and dried them, and Andrew gave her a sharp look, took the tray from her and handed it to another girl, asking her to take them over to the man in charge of pouring out drinks.

'As for you, you are to sit down and stay down,' Andrew told Leonie firmly. He looked behind her and calmly said to some people lounging around on the sofa, 'Would you mind getting off there? Leonie needs to put her feet up.'

They scrambled up at once. 'Sure, Doc!'

'Oh, no, really...' Leonie began to protest, but Andrew manoeuvred her backwards and down on to the sofa.

'Feet up!' he ordered, and with a flushed face she obeyed, frowning a little because she hated being the centre of attention, and everyone was watching them.

'You aren't going to have the baby any minute, are you?' asked someone.

'Certainly not,' said Andrew. 'But she has been on her feet for far too long, and has done far too much this evening. Now it's someone else's turn to fetch and carry.'

People drifted away, probably afraid they would be asked to do some work, and Andrew sat down on the end of the sofa, lifting Leonie's feet on to his lap, and, to her embarrassed amazement, taking off her shoes.

'Angela says you're looking for somewhere cheap to live after the baby is born,' he said as he almost absent-mindedly began to massage one of her feet, his long fingers deft and soothing.

She nodded, grimacing. 'Which is like looking for gold-dust in the street!'

He laughed. 'Don't I know it! When we were all students it was hopeless finding anywhere cheap to live if we couldn't live in at the hospital doctors quarters. Look, are you determined to find somewhere around here? I mean, would you consider moving out of London?'

She looked quickly at him, her heart leaping. 'Why? I mean, yes... I mean, I'd consider anything... you don't mean you know somewhere...somewhere I might be able to afford?'

He hesitated, his face wry. 'Well, don't get your hopes up too high—it is just an idea, it might not be possible. It's just that...well...my mother doesn't usually take lodgers, but my father died five months ago, and she is living alone in their house, and she might consider letting you move into part of the house.'

Leonie drew a sharp, excited breath and he shook his head at her. 'I said, don't get too hopeful. I haven't spoken to her. It only occurred to me this evening. I have to go and visit my mother tomorrow; she's lonely on her own, she's always ringing me up and begging me to come and see her, and I was wondering about the future because I can't keep driving back and forth, but she is too old to get a job, or move...'

'How old is she?' asked Leonie.

'Sixty-four,' said Andrew. 'Frankly, I don't know what to do—I don't seem to have any spare time any more. If I'm not working I'm driving to see my mother. Angela is getting quite bad-tempered about it, and, I must admit, I am, too—I'd like at least a few hours for my own life every week. On the other hand, I feel I have to do something to help my mother. She needs company, something to take her mind off her own troubles.'

'Where does she live?'

'Deepest Essex—a village some miles from the Thames estuary, near Burnham,' he said. 'That's the problem. If you kept your job here it would mean hours of travelling, but I'm sure you could get a job somewhere down there. Of course, I can't speak for my mother. I know she is thinking of letting the flat—the rent would be a help for her. But she would have to see you and make up her own mind.'

'Of course,' Leonie said eagerly.

'Would you like me to talk to her, ask if she'll see you?'

'Yes, please!' How could he doubt it?

He smiled at her, reading her expression while his long fingers still kept busy massaging her feet. It was an amazingly soothing feeling, and she loved it. 'OK, then,' he said. 'I'll talk to her. When could you go there? Could you come down with me on Saturday morning?'

'Yes, of course!' Leonie breathed. She would have agreed to any arrangement, and somehow got the time off, but Saturday would, undoubtedly, be the easiest day to go. It wouldn't involve asking permission of her boss, or having to work overtime to make up for the time lost.

Angela suddenly arrived beside the sofa, eyeing them coldly. 'What are you two up to? You've been whispering away in this corner for hours—what are you talking about?' Then before they could answer she asked even more crossly, 'And are you some kind of foot fetishist, Andrew? Why have you got Leonie's feet on your lap; why are you sitting there stroking and fondling them? Goodness knows what people are thinking!'

'Who cares what people think?' Andrew asked lightly, obviously resenting Angela's suspicions, and Leonie looked from one to the other, very upset at the thought of causing trouble between them.

'Angie, don't be silly! Andrew was only being kind,' she hurriedly said, removing her feet from Andrew's hands and swinging her legs down to the floor.

'Oh, kind is he?' Angela asked with a cynical expression.

'Yes!' Leonie was very pink. 'Oh, come on... look at me! I'm the size of a baby elephant at the moment—you couldn't suspect Andrew of fancying me in my condition!'

Angela didn't look too sure about that.

'Anyway,' Leonie said, 'He may have found me a flat... isn't that wonderful! And he was giving my feet a massage because...'

She broke off, not knowing quite why Andrew had been massaging her feet, and it was Andrew who solemnly explained.

'Her ankles had swollen up with all this trudging about with trays of food and drink, Angel. She shouldn't have been on her feet for such a long time—she should take better care of herself, and rest more, until the baby arrives.'

'Hmm . . .' Angela said, not quite a hundred per cent convinced, but deciding to let that one go. 'And what is all this about a flat? What flat? Where?'

When Andrew told her she made a face. 'But it will mean leaving London . . . going away from all her friends . . . me, for instance . . . She's a Londoner; she won't like it in the country. And I'll miss her.'

Leonie smiled affectionately at her. 'I'll miss you, too, Angela, and all my friends—but I think I am going to have to leave London, you know. It's the only way I can make this situation work.'

'Not the only way,' Angela said drily. 'There is always Giles Kent.'

'I wouldn't even consider accepting any help from him!' Leonie said with angry force, and the other two fell silent, watching her.

Andrew rang next evening to say that his mother had agreed to meet her and discuss the possibility of Leonie's moving into the flat.

'But nothing is decided yet, remember,' Andrew stressed. 'If my mother feels you two could get on, she may agree, but on the other hand she may not be able to face sharing her home with a stranger. I'll pick you up on Saturday morning at ten, and drive you down to

meet her. She suggests we all have lunch together—she enjoys cooking and giving hospi-
tality. We'll arrive there at around midday, have
lunch, then you two can talk while I go for a
walk. There's a train back in the late afternoon, and I'll drive you to the station to catch
it.'

Leonie was very nervous about meeting
Andrew's mother, but she need not have been.
Mrs Colpitt was as warm and friendly as her
son; a small, grey-haired, energetic woman
Leonie found it very easy to talk to and easy to
like.

'It would be nice to have some company,' she
said frankly. 'Some days I don't see another
living soul, unless I walk down to the village
shop and talk to Mrs Dawlish, or a neighbour.
But this flat is self-contained; you'll have your
own front door—come and look at it now, see
what you think.'

It was a cosy little flat; Leonie would have her
own kitchen and a tiny sitting-room cum dining-room, and bedroom and a diminutive bathroom.

'It's wonderful,' she said, and, within half an
hour, it was all settled. Leonie would move into
the flat in three weeks' time. Her maternity leave
began then, so she would not need to look for a
new job for some months and could take time to
settle into the flat, and into the village. She

would have to change doctors and make a new arrangement with the local maternity hospital, Andrew pointed out as he drove her to the station later that day.

'It's vital to do that as soon as possible, as they may well be fully booked already!' he warned.

She nodded soberly. 'I'll make sure to do that at once, then.'

On the platform she turned to him and said gratefully, 'I don't know how to thank you, Andrew. You don't know how worried I've been; I really didn't know how I was going to cope—and now everything is so different suddenly, all because of you.'

A faint flush in his face, he said gruffly, 'That's OK, it was just an idea I had...glad it's worked out...'

Leonie stood on tiptoe and kissed him quickly, on the cheek, as the train roared into the station. 'Thank you,' she whispered, then turned and climbed into the nearest carriage and settled in a window-seat, waving to Andrew as the train began to move again.

On the Sunday morning she got up late and had a light breakfast, then sat down to write a list of everything she must do before she moved. She had got into the habit of thinking she had plenty of time to arrange everything, but suddenly there were only three more weeks before she left London and her job, and all the familiar places and faces. Her life was about to change drastically forever, she thought, staring down at the sheet of paper on which she had written her list.

A little shiver ran down her spine. She felt scared for an instant, facing the unknown future. Then she lifted her chin and sat up straight. She would cope. She had been telling herself that for months now. She could cope—with anything. And she would.

The doorbell jangled and she jumped. Who could that be? Angela, she thought, relaxing and smiling as she got heavily to her feet and made her way to the door, one hand supporting her back. She had tried to ring Angela last night, to tell her what had been decided, but Angela had been at the theatre and hadn't got back until late, by which time Leonie had been asleep for ages. She went to bed early these days, although her sleep was often patchy, since she kept waking up and then going to sleep again during the night.

Opening the door, she began cheerfully, 'Andrew is a darling! It's all arranged...' Then her voice died away as she stared into Giles Kent's hard grey eyes.

'What is?' he asked curtly, frowning, and Leonie bit her lip, so taken aback that she couldn't help stammering.

'Oh, I thought you were Angela.'

'As you see, I'm not,' he said drily. 'What is all arranged? Are you going out today?'

'No, but...' Her voice trailed away uneasily, she flushed, and his black brows rose sharply.

'But what? You're making me very curious.' He took a step forward and Leonie reluctantly had to stand back and let him enter her flat, although she didn't feel strong enough to confront Giles Kent this morning.

He wandered into the flat, and Leonie closed the front door, hurriedly thinking—should she tell him she planned to leave London and move into the country? She wasn't sure she wanted him to know anything about her life; she wanted to make a clean break and get away from him and all the unhappy memories he brought back.

When she followed him into the sitting-room she realised she did not need to make that decision anyway. He had picked up her list and was studying it, his brows together.

Suddenly swinging round to face her, he bit out, 'What is all this?'

'I've found a new flat,' she said huskily. 'I'm moving in there in three weeks' time, when I begin my maternity leave, and I was just making a list of all the things I have to do first.'

'Where is this new flat?' Giles demanded, and, before she could answer that, added in an icy voice, 'And who the hell is Andrew?'

CHAPTER FIVE

LEONIE was confused into flushing and stammering. 'H...he...it...it's his flat!'

Giles stiffened, his eyes narrowing on her. 'His flat?' he repeated in a deep, harsh voice. 'Are you telling me you're moving in with this man?'

'No!' she denied, going quite crimson. 'Of course not! You're confusing me! What I meant was that the flat was Andrew's...'

'What's his surname?' Giles bit out.

'Colpitt,' she said crossly, wishing he would stop talking to her in that hostile voice. She always felt as if she were on the witness stand and he was a prosecuting counsel who did not believe a word she said. Even now, his hard face had a disbelieving look. 'Andrew Colpitt,' she expanded. 'The flat is his, but he isn't living in it at the moment. He is a doctor; he lives in at a London hospital where he works.'

'Is that where you met him?' Giles flicked a glance over her heavily pregnant body, frowning. 'Is he your maternity doctor?'

'No, we were introduced by a friend, who had told Andrew I had a problem finding somewhere to live, so he offered to let me take over his flat for a while, until I can find somewhere of my own. He doesn't use it at the moment. You see, the flat is in Essex, right on the far side of Essex, near the Thames estuary, between Malden and Burnham——'

'That's barely twenty miles from us,' Giles interrupted, and she hadn't thought of that until that moment.

'I suppose it is,' she said, taken aback. She had only visited his home a few times, and had no happy memories of Warlock House, although it was a very handsome building set among lovely gardens, and the Essex countryside surrounding it was beautiful. Malcolm had adored his home, but she had never felt welcome, or at home, there. How odd that she hadn't realised how close to it she would be if she moved down to Andrew's village! Or perhaps it wasn't odd at all. Maybe she had deliberately blanked out the realisation that she would be so close to Warlock House?

'What about your job?' asked Giles. 'Surely you won't commute from there?'

She shook her head. 'No, of course not— that's what I was trying to explain—why Andrew doesn't use the flat: it's too far for him to be able to commute back and forth, but that won't matter to me because I start my maternity leave shortly, so I won't be working for quite some time, anyway.'

'Of course,' said Giles slowly.

'I could have stayed here until the baby had arrived, but I'd have to find a flat somewhere else after that, so when Andrew offered to let me have his flat while he isn't using it, I jumped at it.'

Giles was watching her with a black frown. 'And what about when he does want to use it?' he asked, his mouth crooked with cynicism. 'Or hadn't you thought of that? Don't tell me his offer is just altruistic, because I don't believe it. What if he arrives one day and expects to move back in? What will you do then?'

'You don't understand! Oh, I haven't explained this very well,' Leonie began, and Giles interrupted coldly,

'I think I'm getting the picture!'

'No, you're not!' she snapped, glaring at him. 'You're just jumping to all the wrong conclusions. Deliberately. You like insulting me. You want to believe the worst of me, you always have!'

His frown deepened and the hard eyes were ice floes. 'I'm stating the obvious. I offered my help, and you turned me down—but you're taking this man's help. Why? Is he an old friend?'

She bit her lip, hesitated, then had to be honest and shook her head. 'But that has nothing to do with it,' she muttered, and Giles smiled icily.

'No? So, how long have you known him?'

'A . . . a little while,' she said, her eyes avoiding his, not liking to say she had only met Andrew a week ago.

'A little while? How long is that? A few months?' His eyes intently read her expressions. 'A few weeks?' Leonie didn't answer, didn't look at him, and he added scathingly, 'but you are accepting his help, when you turned down mine?'

'That's different,' she said, suddenly very angry, her blue eyes moving to his taut face, her chin lifted in defiance. 'I would rather die than take anything from you or your family! You know why. And what I do is none of your business—I don't know what makes you think you have the right to cross-question me as if I were in the witness box and you were the prosecution lawyer. Or the judge! Yes, you think you're entitled to sit in judgement on me, don't you? I've always felt that that was what you were doing.'

Her voice had risen; she was trembling with a peculiar, volatile mixture of feelings: she was nervous because she was telling Giles what she thought of him, she was angry, as always when she thought of the way he and his family had treated her, and she felt a hurt resentment because he always thought the worst of her.

'You shouldn't get so upset—it must be bad for the baby,' was all Giles said, and that made her want to scream.

'Oh, go away!' she threw at him furiously, very flushed. 'I don't want you in my life. Will you stop turning up out of the blue? We have nothing to say to each other, we never have had. We don't like each other, and I never want to see you again.'

That, at least, finally hit home. She saw his grey eyes flash like summer lightning, brilliant and dangerous. A dark flush invaded his face, too. His mouth was tightly reined, and he barely parted his lips to snap back at her. 'That's too bad, because you're going to have to see me again! I've been consulting my lawyers——'

'Lawyers!' she muttered, paling.

'Yes, and we had a very useful discussion,' Giles said with an angry sort of triumph, watching the alarm in her eyes. 'Malcolm left a will, you know. He made it before he even met you, but it is still valid, and it names me as his executor, which, you must realise, means that I take charge of all legal matters arising from his affairs. He didn't leave a fortune, but he did leave quite a large sum, and, of course, he also leaves a share of the family estate. That would have passed to me, but, after a good deal of consideration, our lawyers believe that your child will have a perfectly valid claim on his or her father's estate . . .'

'I'm not going to claim anything!' Leonie protested, but Giles overrode her, his tone insistent.

'A claim, which, as the child's uncle, as well as the executor of the estate, I shall certainly see is admitted, whether you like it or not. Malcolm's child isn't going to be cheated out of his or her rights. In any case, sooner or later this matter would have to be cleared up. You may not want the money, but when the child comes of age I've no doubt he or she will take a very different view, and it will be much easier to sort it out now.'

Angrily, Leonie said, 'Well, I can't stop you, I suppose, but I don't want any of the money. Put it in a trust fund or something.'

'We could do that; indeed, that is undoubtedly what will be done, since the child is not yet even born,' Giles agreed blandly, and something in his tone disturbed her. 'Which, of course, raises other important questions.'

'What?' she warily asked, every nerve in her body prickling with a sense of danger.

'Custody and access,' said Giles, and she went white.

'What?'

'Well, obviously, as executor of my brother's estate I would also be executor of the trust fund which would be set up for his child, and that would make me legal guardian of his child, the heir to that estate,' Giles said in a calm, reasonable voice which was like a knife twisting inside her.

'Malcolm didn't make you the baby's guardian; he didn't even know I was having a child...' she cried, her mouth dry.

'No,' agreed Giles coolly, smiling. 'Naturally, he did not, but if he had known he was going to be a father, and if he had had second sight and realised he was going to die, I am certain he would have made provision for me to be the child's guardian, just as he made me the executor of his will—Malcolm trusted me. He knew I would look after his interests, and, since the child is in a sense part of his estate, as the main beneficiary of it, especially since you insist that the money is put into a trust fund, which I shall have to administer for the child, I shall obviously become the child's legal guardian.'

'No!' Leonie whispered, her legs shaking under her so that she had to sit down on the nearest chair.

Giles hurriedly crossed the room. 'Are you OK? You aren't going to faint, are you?'

She shook her head, closing her eyes against the penetrating probe of those grey eyes.

'Can I get you anything? A cup of tea? Brandy?' he asked, sounding husky.

'C...could you get me a drink of water?' she asked shakily, and he went at once, returning a second later with a glass which he pushed into her hand, his cool fingers closing around her own to help her lift the glass to her mouth, as if she were a child.

Leonie drank thirstily, keeping her eyes closed yet very conscious of him beside her, his long, lean body a physical and mental threat she could not face for the moment. Perhaps he would go away if he believed she was ill?

When she stopped drinking, he removed the glass and stood up, but only to say, 'How do you feel now?'

'I would like to lie down for an hour, so if you don't mind leaving...?' Leonie said softly.

There was a silence, then he said drily, 'Can we finish our discussion first? I think you should be aware of the legal steps I'm taking.'

'Legal steps?' she repeated, her eyes flying open.

She was surprised to find him still so close. He stared down at her, his grey eyes cool and determined. 'I intend to become the child's legal guardian, by virtue of being my brother's executor, and I am sure the law will uphold my claim.'

'I'm the baby's mother!' she denied fiercely, and he smiled, a faint twist of the mouth which had no humour in it.

'You have no money and no home of your own, you will shortly have no job, and you will have to live on state benefit. And, even if you get another job after the birth, you will earn very little, and you will have to leave the child with someone else.'

She stared at him bleakly, unable to contradict any of that, and he nodded at her.

'Yes, it is all true, isn't it? I, on the other hand, have a great deal of money, and can offer my brother's child a wonderful future, the sort of life he or she would have had if Malcolm had lived and married you.'

'Money isn't everything. I shall love my baby, and I shall make a good home for it,' she muttered, tears at the back of her eyes.

'I'm sure you would try, but it would be hard, for both of you, and it doesn't have to be! You are being stubborn and selfish.'

'Selfish!' Leonie broke out, hating him.

'What else can one call it? You aren't thinking about what is best for the baby, you're only concerned with your own ego. You resent me because I didn't want you to marry my brother, so you are refusing to let me help, even though that means your child will suffer.'

She bit down into her lip, unable to argue about that.

Giles watched her for a moment in silence, then said coolly, 'Now, we can go to court to argue this out, but I assure you that I would win.'

She stared at him dumbly, believing it. Giles always won. Hadn't Malcolm told her that, over and over again? He always won, and he would win this time. She could feel that he was already winning. She simply did not know how to argue with him.

'I am not disputing your right, as the child's mother, to have custody,' he said after a pause to see if she would speak. 'But I feel that it may be necessary to register an equal right, legally, as its guardian, to determine the place of its abode, its education, and so on—and to make sure of access, visiting rights, for myself and my mother.'

'I've already said that your mother can see the baby!' Leonie protested, disturbed by all this talk about law and rights. Was he moving towards claiming the child, taking it away from her? Could he do that? She must see a lawyer herself, at once—but how on earth was she to afford one? She would go to the Citizen's Advice Bureau and ask them for help. She might be able to get a lawyer's opinion under the legal aid system. She bitterly wished she knew more about such things, but she had never had to worry about the law before.

'Ah, but it is always wise to have these things in writing, in a form of legal, contractual agreement,' said Giles. 'You might change your mind later, or deny you had ever promised that.'

'I wouldn't!'

He shrugged. 'All the same, we would like it in black and white. And there's another thing— the child can inherit Malcolm's estate, but it will not carry his name, and that makes my mother unhappy. She wants the baby to be a Kent.'

Leonie hesitated, sighing. 'Well, I did think of that—and I would like Malcolm's baby to have Malcolm's surname, but it could be embarrassing if we had different surnames.'

'That's true,' said Giles, 'but there is a way round that.'

She looked up at him blankly. 'Oh?'

'Yes,' he said without expression. 'You could marry me before the baby is born, and then it will, legally, take the Kent name.'

She stood there, frozen on the spot, staring at him and not really sure whether it had been a joke or not, or even whether she had heard him correctly.

'That isn't funny!' she whispered at last.

'It wasn't meant to be!'

'You can't be serious.' She knew he couldn't mean it. He hadn't wanted her to marry his brother—he certainly wouldn't dream of marrying her himself.

'Very serious,' Giles said in that cool, level voice which sounded so matter-of-fact that somehow it made her feel more and more as if she were trapped in a weird, surrealist dream— or a nightmare. 'You see, it wouldn't really be good enough to simply register the baby under the surname Kent,' Giles added. 'My mother is afraid about the future—if you married someone else, for instance!'

'I wouldn't——' she began, and he spoke over her, his tone hard.

'You may say that now, but you're very young, you'll get over Malcolm's death and you'll meet someone else. This doctor, for instance . . . Dr Colpitt . . . I've no doubt he must be interested in you, or he wouldn't have been so generous in offering to let you use his flat.'

'He isn't interested in me at all!' Leonie denied immediately, but Giles again spoke over her, his voice harsh.

'Perhaps you simply haven't realised how he feels yet! And, even if you aren't interested in Dr Colpitt, there will be someone one day. You're beautiful, and you're very feminine. You aren't cut out for the single life, even if you do have a child. You'll marry sooner or later, and your new husband might insist that the baby take his name, might refuse us access, might even try to get his hands on the baby's money. We have to protect our rights, and those of the child.'

'You're crazy!' Leonie burst out, and Giles suddenly laughed, startling her even more.

'On the contrary, I'm talking sound common sense,' he drawled. 'We are not going to allow you to marry someone else and give Malcolm's child into the control of a stranger. And, as there isn't much time left before the birth, I suggest we get married in a register office as soon as possible.'

Leonie was gasping like a landed fish. Breathlessly, she managed to gulp out, 'I've never heard anything so——'

'I'll make all the necessary arrangements,' Giles interrupted her splutterings.

'You must be out of your mind!'

'I suggest we only invite close family to attend. Your mother. Mine. My sister and her family. No friends, not even your pal Angela.'

Leonie shouted at him, since he didn't appear to have heard her until now. 'Listen to me, will you? I am not going to marry you!'

'Any preference as to the location?' he calmly enquired. 'London? That would probably be best; it would arouse less interest than it might if we got married in Essex, near my home. We don't want a lot of gossip and people turning up to stare.'

'I don't believe this is happening,' Leonie said to the ceiling.

'Oh, by the way, I shall require you to sign a pre-marital contract,' said Giles casually. 'Quite common, these days, I assure you, but under these very unusual circumstances I must protect myself, you understand——'

'I won't marry you!' Leonie yelled.

'And of course I shall have the legal documents referring to Malcolm's child drawn up at the same time, so that there is no legal confusion later as to whose child it is . . .'

Leonie got up and said through almost closed lips, very quietly and firmly, 'I am moving out of this flat and going away, and whatever you say or do won't make any difference—I am not marrying you, I won't even see you again if I can help it, and you are going to have to take me to court to get access to my baby, because after this I am going to fight you, whatever it costs me.'

'It will cost you your child!' Giles icily promised, and she stood there, appalled, staring back at him.

'You couldn't——'

'I would,' he said, and she believed him. A wave of chill shock flowed up over her whole body. She was trapped. He had spelt it out for her now—whatever she tried to do, wherever she turned, or tried to run, he would stop her, he would force her to do as he and his family wished. She was carrying his brother's child, and he meant to control it—and her. It was his nature to impose control, he understood only too well how to do it, and he terrified her.

'You will marry me,' he said, and she felt so threatened that she turned to run away like a scared child, not even knowing where she was going or what she meant to do.

Not that it mattered much what she intended, because Giles caught her before she had got very far. His hands fastened on her shoulders and dragged her round to face him.

'Get your hands off me!' she shakily threw at him. 'I wouldn't marry you if you were the last man in the world! I hate you!'

For a second he was very still, staring down at her, his face locked in a taut mask she couldn't read until she suddenly saw that his grey eyes glittered with anger, his mouth was hard with temper. A shudder of dismay and foreboding went through her.

'That's too bad,' he said through his teeth. 'Because, hate me or not, you are going to marry me, Leonie, so you had better get used to the idea.'

'No,' she whispered, her eyes held hypnotically by the power of his demanding stare. 'I couldn't marry you! I can't even bear it when you touch me!'

As soon as the words left her lips she wished she could call them back; she knew it had been a stupid, reckless thing to say, and his expression underlined her own instincts.

'Can't you? Well, let's see, shall we?' he bit out, and her nerves leapt at the furious flash of his icy grey eyes.

His head began to lower towards her, and she cried out in shock and alarm, 'No! Don't...'

His mouth took hers with driving force and her head went back under the insistence of that demand. She fought him, twisting and turning in his arms, but he pulled her closer, the warmth of his body touching her from breast to thigh, his hands moving on her, up and down her back, under her hair, caressing her nape, her throat, her breasts. She couldn't breathe, she was trembling violently, heat mounting inside her as his exploration of her body became more and more intimate, his kiss deeper and more urgent.

She hadn't expected to feel this way; she was so appalled by her own physical reaction that she couldn't go on fighting him. Her body was swamped by an intense desire, her eyes closed, her hands went flat against him, touching his body and feeling the warmth of him through his clothes, beating up into her palms and through her own body until they were almost one being, the rhythm of their lives merging in a fierce, heavy beat. Her back arched as she yielded limply, swaying against him like a flower too heavy to stand upright. Her lips parted, trembling, under the hot pressure of his kiss.

When Giles finally lifted his head she was almost fainting, but she felt him looking down at her, the power of his will forcing her lids to flutter upwards.

He stared into her eyes and she stared back helplessly, for a second unable to think because passion had drowned out everything else in her head.

She thought for that instant that Giles looked as shaken as she felt, and her trembling intensified, her bones seemed to have turned to jelly. Was he feeling like this? What was happening to them?

Then his eyes flicked down, noting the tremors in her body, he frowned, and his mouth twisted. He looked up again, into her eyes, and gave her a mocking little smile. 'What were you saying?'

She felt her skin burning and looked away, hating him, but now hating herself, too. How could she have let him do that to her? He had deliberately set out to shame and humiliate her, show her that if he chose to exert the sex appeal Angela had kept talking about she wouldn't be able to resist him, and she had let him prove his point.

She pulled herself together somehow and managed a husky defiance. 'Just because I couldn't fight you doesn't mean I enjoyed it! I didn't! I hated every minute of it and if you ever lay a hand on me again I'll kill you!'

A dark flush invaded his face, too. His brows met, his grey eyes threatened.

'You will marry me, though!' he told her curtly. 'Or take the consequences, and, I assure you, Leonie, I will win. I always do.'

She believed him, and fell silent. What option did she have? She was going to be forced into this marriage, whether she liked it or not.

'You can't!' Angela said, her face shocked and incredulous. 'You've always said how much you hated the man! Now you're saying you're going to... Oh, I don't believe it. It's crazy! You can't marry him!'

'You were the one who said I should go to him for help!' Leonie muttered in grim amusement, although why she should find it funny that Angela was so shaken she did not know. There was nothing amusing about any of this— Angela was right: it was crazy to even consider marrying Giles Kent.

Crossly Angela snapped, 'You know what I meant! I still think the Kent family ought to help you. The baby is Malcolm's too, even if you weren't actually married yet. You were going to be, and I'm sure you could make some sort of legal claim on them—and heaven knows they have enough money! They wouldn't miss it if they made some sort of financial settlement on you. They could afford to be generous.'

'The money is the whole point,' Leonie said bitterly. 'You're right, I would have a good legal claim on them. They have found out that the baby would be entitled to claim its father's share of the family money. That's what their lawyers have told them, and it's scared the life out of them.'

Angela grew flushed with excitement, her lips parting in a gasp. 'But that's marvellous! You won't have any more worries if——'

'You don't understand!' Leonie interrupted brusquely. 'They have no intention of settling money on me—and, in fact, I told him I didn't even want their money, but he doesn't believe me, doesn't trust me. He says I may say that now, but how do they know I won't change my mind later? Anyway, they're going to set up a trust fund for the baby, and he is going to be the executor of it, because Malcolm's will made him his executor.'

Angela's frown deepened. 'Well, that's good, isn't it? You know that that's what Malcolm would have wanted. You can't resent Malcolm's baby inheriting his father's money?'

'No, of course I don't!'

'Then...' Angela looked bewildered. 'You've lost me. You said Giles was blackmailing you into marrying him! Now you say he agrees that the baby should inherit Malcolm's share of the business.'

'I've just explained—it will all go into a trust fund for the baby, and Giles intends to manage the fund. But he's afraid that I may marry someone who will come along, one day, and try to take over running the fund as the child's stepfather. He wants to make quite sure that can never happen, so he is marrying me himself to get control of my baby and keep the money in the Kent family.'

Angela's eyes rounded, and she chewed on her lower lip thoughtfully, a calculating expression in her face. 'Well, it makes sense, I suppose.'

'To a computer!' Leonie spat, infuriated. 'Or to a man with all the emotions of a computer!'

Angela shrugged, eyeing her with curiosity. 'Don't do it if you really hate him that much! After all, he can't force you to marry him!'

'He can,' said Leonie.

Angela laughed scornfully. 'Not in this day and age. What is he going to do? Drag you to the altar?'

'Start legal proceedings to take the baby away as soon as it is born,' said Leonie.

Angela gasped. 'You're kidding!'

'That's what he threatens. He would ask for custody on the grounds that the baby is the heir to a large trust fund, and I am not in a position to bring it up properly.'

'He would never get a court to agree!'

Leonie smiled wearily. 'Well, maybe not. But what if he did? These things do happen. Rich people can afford top barristers, they can manipulate the system. And, let's face it, the Kent family can offer the baby far more than I can, in a material sense. He pointed out that I'd have to go out to work, leaving the baby with someone else, and I wouldn't have much money, especially as I refuse to take any from him, and I can't afford a very nice flat, or even a full-time, properly qualified nanny. Oh, thousands of unmarried mothers do manage to look after a baby and have a job, but nobody says it's easy, and a court might feel that it would be in the baby's best interests for it to live with its grandmother.'

Angela was sober now. She grimaced. 'Yes, I see what you mean!'

'I must get in touch with Andrew and explain, and apologise!' Leonie said on a long sigh. 'He has been so kind, and his mother was, too. I would have loved to live in that flat. Oh, why is life so...so unpredictable? Why do things keep happening to me like this? So suddenly, I mean, out of the blue. Just when I think I've finally worked something out, got my life into shape—wham! Fate hits me with something I couldn't possibly expect. Just when I was going to marry Malcolm...' Her voice broke. She bit down on her lower lip, gesturing, tears in her eyes. 'Oh, you know...it all blew up in my face!' She ran a hand over her eyes. 'And now this. One minute everything seemed to be falling into place so nicely...all my worries dealt with...and I felt so marvellous for a while, thinking I was going to be moving down there, able to relax for a while before the baby came, have my baby peacefully and take my time looking for a job near by—and then fate sees to it that it all blows up in my face again.'

'You mean Giles Kent sees to it!' Angela said drily.

Leonie nodded grimly, getting up out of her chair with some difficulty, her hand on her aching back. She hadn't slept much the night before; partly because she had been lying awake anxiously thinking about what Giles had said to her, and partly because the baby had been very lively, kicking violently all night. Even before it was born, she had the feeling this baby was going to be a typical Kent: obstinate, overbearing, determined to get its own way.

'I think he only decided to marry me after I'd told him I was moving into Andrew's flat,' she muttered. 'He suspected I might be getting involved with Andrew, and he wouldn't believe me when I told him I wasn't romantically involved with anyone.' She smoothed a hand down over her heavy body, looking down at it with a rueful expression. 'As if it were likely! What man would look twice at me when I look like a barrage balloon?'

Angela didn't answer the rhetorical question. Instead, she said with sudden interest, 'What are you going to wear?'

Leonie laughed shortly, giving her a wry, impatient, but affectionate look, because it was so typical of Angela to be distracted by thoughts of clothes.

'That's the last thing on my mind! Nobody will be dressing up, anyway. If anybody comes!'

'I'll come!' Angela said indignantly. 'And I'll be dressing up, you can bet on it!'

'I'm sorry, I can't invite you—Giles says no friends,' Leonie told her apologetically. 'Just family, and as few of them as possible. But you wouldn't want to go, anyway—you won't be missing much. This isn't a real wedding, Angela. It is just a sham; a legal arrangement. I get the feeling he wants to be able to get out of it as easily as possible later, so he's making sure not too many people know about it.'

'Well, he isn't stopping me from turning up to see you get married,' Angela muttered, scowling. 'What's he going to do afterwards? Hide you somewhere until after the baby has been born?'

Leonie went pale. She hadn't thought about 'afterwards' yet. Now she did, and she did not like what she suspected the future might hold for her. Questions crowded into her head, and while she was thinking about the answers Angela began to ask the questions aloud, in her practical, direct way.

'Where are you going to live, for instance? At Warlock House? With that old gorgon of a mother? And what do you mean ... not a real wedding? Are you saying you won't be living as man and wife?'

Leonie didn't know, she could only shake her head helplessly and shrug.

Angela gazed at her disbelievingly. 'You're out of your skull if you go through with this!' she told her, and she was right, thought Leonie.

She must be mad to be marrying a man who not only did not love her, but didn't even like her. In fact, she had often felt he hated her. There was a darkness behind Giles Kent's grey eyes; something fierce and angry and threatening. It had been there from the beginning. She had always been aware of it; a taut thread had stretched between them whenever they were together, a consciousness, one of the other, which frightened her. She had been able to cope so long as she did not see too much of him—but she went into panic every time she thought of becoming his wife, being alone with him, at his mercy.

CHAPTER SIX

THEY were married three weeks later, in a brief civil ceremony, which was over so fast that Leonie both at the time and afterwards felt as if it had been a dream.

It was all so functional, so banal. She wore a cream wool two-piece suit. Giles wore grey. Neither of them smiled. Their voices murmured in the quiet room, and they went through the motions as commanded without even looking at each other.

Behind them, in a row, sat a handful of people. His mother, his sister and her husband, Leonie's mother, Angela and Andrew. There were so few of them in the room that Leonie could actually hear them all breathing, even above the sound of rain.

It seemed very apt that it should be raining. London in the rain had such a bleak look, depressed and depressing—the grey-blue slate roofs of tall office blocks opposite shone wet, bare wintry trees bowed in resignation before the attack of the wind, and there was a sound of tyres on wet roads, the running of water in gutters. People huddled in doorways, ran for buses, hurried along the slippery pavements hunched in their coats.

There was no wedding reception. Giles had ruled that that would be pointless, in the circumstances. He whisked her away without allowing her to exchange more than a few stiff words with anyone, and she was glad about that, even while she resented his high-handed assumption that he merely had to give an order for her to meekly obey.

'What dreadful weather, isn't it?' his sister, Linda, said, trying not to stare at her. They had not met since before Malcolm's death, and, although she knew Linda had been told she was pregnant, it was obviously still a shock to actually see the evidence of it.

'Were the roads difficult on your way here?' Leonie asked without caring whether Linda answered or not. What else was there to say? Anything that was really on their minds had to be left unsaid as too dangerous.

She had said something to Mrs Kent, but she had hardly known what she was saying. Mrs Kent had answered her, but their eyes had never met. Perhaps they had both been thinking about that other wedding-day, which had never happened? It would all have been so different on that day. Not a brief, muttered exchange in a shabby London office, between people dressed as if for a day at work, but a sacred ritual, with everything that that meant—a bride in white, a church, the peal of an organ, crowds of smiling wedding guests, a groom waiting at an altar, faith, hope and love exchanged along with the rings they gave each other.

How could she have met Malcolm's mother's eyes when they were both remembering what might have been?

Yet Leonie had been very aware of the older woman's pallor and the fact that she was horribly thin. She had never been anything but slim, an elegant woman with a good figure. Now she was fleshless, and as tense as a tightened bow. Malcolm's death had drained his mother, too, of life; had depleted her, left her looking some ten years older.

Angela had come to hug her, half crying, and Leonie had tried not to cry, too, hurriedly turning to shake Andrew's hand.

He made some conventionally polite remark, and she said, 'Thank you,' huskily.

Leonie had been too angry to talk to her own mother, whose triumphant glitter she had seen out of the corner of her eye as she'd walked into the room. Martha was tense, too, but with excitement, exaltation. She was there to watch her daughter marry into a very rich family, and she was walking on air.

She looked superb, of course; her pale hair in a French pleat at the back of her head, her face perfectly made-up, her slender body sheathed in coral silk, her small, thin feet in shoes that matched that shade exactly. She wore a tiny white silk hat perched on the top of her head, a fine veil falling over her eyes, giving her an air of mystery.

Leonie wondered how much the elegant clothes had cost her. A small fortune, no doubt, and Giles was probably going to have to foot the bill. Martha would make sure of that. It was humiliating, and Leonie almost hated her mother at that moment.

'We're leaving now,' Giles had said, though, before she had had to decide whether or not to publicly ignore her mother, and a moment later she found herself walking away, his hand under her elbow, steering her.

A sleek grey limousine had been waiting at the kerb, outside. Giles had helped her into the back, slid into the seat beside her. Then they were moving away, through the softly falling rain, through the grey London streets, and Leonie had leaned back, closing her eyes wearily, glad to escape from the necessity to be polite, to talk, to smile, to pretend.

Giles sat beside her, an apparently relaxed figure; a tall, lean man in a smoothly tailored suit, a white carnation in his buttonhole the only evidence that they had been married. He didn't say anything; she barely heard him breathing.

After a few moments she opened her eyes again and gave him a quick, nervous, sidelong look.

'Where are we going?'

'Home,' Giles said, and she had a confused moment of uncertainty about what he meant.

'Home?' she repeated, her voice rising to a question.

'Warlock,' he said, and she couldn't help an instinctive shudder. Warlock House might mean home to him, but she had been unhappy there on her few visits. She had been forced to recognise that Malcolm's family were hostile to her, rejected her, and at some level of her mind she had begun to feel that the house itself rejected her.

Giles frowned, his body half turned towards her, his cold eyes stripping her face of privacy, invading her mind, understanding what she was thinking in a way she found increasingly disturbing.

'It *is* your home now,' he said curtly.

There was anger in his voice, in his face, and she knew why. Giles resented having had to marry her, he hated the idea of bringing her, of all people, home to Warlock as his bride.

She shook her head, her face paler than ever inside its frame of fine silvery hair. 'No. I'll never feel I belong there, or that it is my home. How could I? I'm not really your wife. Our marriage was a crazy piece of legal fiction; it isn't real!'

'Don't deceive yourself!' Giles snarled, brows heavy and black over those icy grey eyes. 'Or anybody else! Don't give anyone any wrong ideas. That guy Colpitt, for instance—I saw the way he looked at you, and the way you almost burst into tears when he was holding your hand. If he so much as shows up at Warlock, I'll set the dogs on him. Just remember this... our marriage is very real, and you not only are my wife, you are going to stay my wife unless, or until, I say otherwise!'

A flood of startled, incredulous pink washed up her face. 'What are you talking about? Andrew?' Her voice broke down into a husky, embarrassed stammer. 'He isn't my... we aren't...'

'Not yet?' sneered Giles coldly, then without warning caught hold of her chin in his long fingers, tipped her head back, and stared down into her wide dark blue eyes.

'He's another guy like Malcolm, isn't he? Easy on the eye, easy to like—a charmer.'

She was startled, incredulous. 'Andrew's nothing like Malcolm!' How could he think he was? 'Malcolm was much better looking, and very different in character,' she denied. There was much more to it than that, though. 'Andrew ... well, he's serious ... a very caring man ...' She didn't want to seem to be criticising Malcolm, especially to Giles, but he had been light-hearted and at times even a little selfish. Andrew was probably a much better man, although he was not as lovable as Malcolm had been.

Giles looked angrily into her eyes, seeming to dive down into them, read the mind behind them. 'You still think about him?' he bit out, and she went white again.

'Damn you! This isn't the time and place to talk about Malcolm!' she muttered.

He shrugged and let go of her. 'No. You're right. Well, remember what I said—if I find Dr Colpitt near you again I won't be so gentlemanly next time.'

She shrank away from him into the corner of the limousine and stared out of the window as they drove east, through London's grimy suburbs, each mile taking them closer to the flat Essex countryside.

What he had just said had shown her suddenly that her memories of Malcolm had changed in some inexplicable, subtle way. Her love for him hadn't so much ended as faded, like a photograph left in the light, the edges blurring, the sharpness softening. She thought of him far less; days passed without Malcolm entering her thoughts, although when he did she still felt a sadness, but without the incredulous, piercing pain, the ache she had once felt.

That was why she had gone white when Giles had asked her if she still thought of Malcolm. It had shaken her to realise she could do so without wanting to cry—when for so long she had dreamt of him and woken in tears. She couldn't have borne it for Giles to know, to read the admission in her face. Her anger had been defensive; ashamed.

She bit her lip, watching the thinning ranks of grey houses at the edge of London as they sped along a motorway leading towards the coast.

Malcolm had only been dead for seven months! Shame washed through her and she closed her eyes. She had believed her heart was broken the day Giles had told her his brother was dead. How could she get over his death this soon? Was that all love meant? Seven months and you forgot?

'Are you OK?' Giles spoke quietly, but he still made her start in shock, her eyes flying open.

She looked round at him. 'What?'

He was pale. He looked into her dark blue eyes, frowning. 'I was afraid you might be feeling ill. You don't look well.'

She relaxed slightly, seeing that his fit of harsh temper was over. He was a strange man and she did not understand him, but when he spoke gently like this she felt she might actually learn to like him.

'I'm a little tired, that's all,' she huskily said. 'It was a bit of an ordeal, after all, the ceremony and so on.'

He nodded. 'Of course. And I'm sorry if I upset you; it was stupid of me to start an argument over nothing. I was feeling rather tense myself, I suppose.'

She gave a faint sigh of relief. 'I understand. It has been a difficult day for both of us.'

They finished the drive to Warlock House in a friendlier silence, each staring out of the window at the countryside they passed through. Essex was not one of the most beautiful counties of England; it was flat and heavily built up in places, but in some of the older villages there were interesting houses and churches; white wood steeples, decorated plastering on house walls, black and white frame houses.

As they drove along narrow, winding, hedge-lined lanes and came within sight of Warlock House, Leonie began to get nervous. Every visit she had made to this house had been fraught and uneasy. She didn't know if she could bear to live there, under the same roof as Giles and his mother, even if it was only for a few months.

She was feeling confused about that now. The marriage had happened so quickly; she hadn't seen much of Giles in the past few weeks and they hadn't talked much about what was to happen after the wedding. What he had said had given her the distinct impression that after the birth of the baby they would make some arrangement—an annulment, maybe, or at any rate a legal separation. He would obviously be the baby's guardian, but she would have custody of her child, and she had vaguely had an idea that she would find a flat, a job, as she had planned before, and someone to look after the baby.

She certainly did not think of the marriage as a real one; as she had said to Giles just now, it was a legal fiction, meant to give Giles more power as the executor of Malcolm's will. She had agreed because of the blackmail Giles had threatened her with, but she had gone through with it without believing in what she was doing.

She didn't feel like a married woman; she didn't feel as if Giles was her husband.

She gave him a startled, confused look sideways. He was staring straight ahead, himself wrapped in thought, his black brows knit, his jawline taut.

For the first time Leonie realised the fact—the man beside her was her husband!

At that instant Giles turned to look at her, as if becoming aware that she was watching him, and Leonie felt hot colour wash up her face.

For a second they stared into each other's eyes, and she heard her own heart beating, fast and loud, echoing in her ears like the sea in a shell, then Giles glanced away and said flatly, 'We're here.'

As the car pulled up outside the house a man hurriedly emerged, buttoning up his black jacket. He opened the door and solicitously, as if she were an invalid, helped Leonie to descend, a polite smile on his thin face.

'Welcome home, madam.'

Leonie murmured a husky, 'Thank you.' She didn't know who he was, and hadn't seen him before.

He flicked an uncertain sideways glance at Giles as he joined them, and she uneasily wondered just what Giles had told people about her and their marriage. Her condition was so obvious; she knew it must be arousing a lot of gossip, and her embarrassment made her flush to her hairline.

'This is George,' said Giles, standing close to her, a frown knitting his brows. 'He and his wife are running the house for us now. Is Marjorie waiting inside, George?'

'Yes, sir.'

'Good. Then come and meet her, Leonie.' Giles put a hand under her elbow and steered her towards the front door.

She went reluctantly. Warlock House had always overawed her. She walked into it now with a sensation of disbelief; after Malcolm's death she had never expected to see it again, yet here she was walking into the house as the wife of Giles Kent himself.

At least his mother wasn't here. She was spending the next week with her daughter, so Leonie would be given a short breathing-space, a little time to get accustomed to living in this house with Giles as her husband.

She swallowed, giving him another sidelong look of confused incredulity. Her husband? Giles Kent?

It made her feel odd to think about it, so she made herself think about her new mother-in-law instead. She was hoping Mrs Kent was less hostile towards her now, but she wasn't yet sure. Only time would tell.

She hadn't seen enough of her new mother-in-law over the past month or so to be able to guess whether or not they were going to get on together. It all depended on how Mrs Kent felt about the baby. If Giles was right, she would be ready to make Leonie welcome for the baby's sake. If he was wrong about his mother's feelings, life was going to be impossible in this house.

'Ah! There you are, Marjorie!' Giles said as a woman hurried towards them from the back of the panelled hall, and Leonie started, turning her attention back to the present.

George's wife, Marjorie, was a woman in her forties, fair and flushed, rather short, but wiry, with lively blue eyes. She very carefully did not notice Leonie's obvious condition, smiling at her and beginning to talk at once in a breathless voice. 'Oh, I'm sorry I wasn't there to welcome you, but I was upstairs, putting the finishing touches to your room, when I heard the car coming up the drive.'

'Not at all,' Leonie shyly murmured, shaking hands.

Marjorie gave Giles an uncertain look. 'I hope everything went off OK? I mean, I hope it was a nice wedding.' She was stammering now, looking confused under Giles's ironic gaze. 'And congratulations . . . best wishes for the future . . .'

'Thank you, Marjorie, that's very kind,' Giles said drily. 'Now, would you show my wife her room? She is tired and would like a rest before lunch.' He glanced down at Leonie. 'I'll see you down here in half an hour, OK?'

'Yes,' she said in a low voice, turning to follow the housekeeper towards the staircase.

Giles had promised her that their marriage would be one in name only; they would not share a room. She was relieved to find he was keeping his word, but at the same time it embarrassed her that everyone should know they were sleeping apart. But in her condition that probably wouldn't surprise anyone! After all, she would have the baby very soon, a matter of a few weeks now!

She gave Marjorie a secret glance, biting her inner lip. What was the other woman really thinking? Leonie was glad she did not know.

Marjorie flung open a door and stood back, smiling. Leonie walked into the room and gave a spontaneous cry of pleasure. 'Oh, it's lovely!'

Marjorie beamed. 'I'm glad you like it.'

It was obvious she had taken trouble over the room; it was immaculate and smelt of roses, a large vase of pink ones which stood on a bedside table next to a glass bowl of fruit. The décor was light and spring-like, green and cream; the antique oak furniture, mostly from the end of the last century, in the art nouveau style, was golden in colour and so highly polished that you could see the room reflected in it.

'Your bathroom is through this door,' Marjorie said, and Leonie looked into the matching room beyond, that too decorated in cream and green; the deep-piled cream carpet identical to that in the bedroom, the green and cream chintz curtains the same, too. Thick, fluffy cream towels, embroidered in dark green with the initial 'K' for Kent, hung over a heated towel-rail. On shelving behind the bath stood rows of jars and bottles full of expensive lotions and bath oils, and the air was scented with perfume.

'What a nice deep bath—and a shower cubicle, too!' she said politely.

'And this is Mr Giles's room,' Marjorie said with a little smile, opening another door.

Leonie felt herself blush and didn't look into the other room, turning away, wishing Marjorie would go now and leave her alone.

As if picking that up, Marjorie said, 'Is there anything I can get you? A cup of tea? Some milk?'

'No, thank you.' Leonie just wanted a little privacy.

'Well, I'll be off, then—I'll turn down the bed for you first.' Before Leonie could protest she deftly stripped the green and cream chintz cover, which matched the curtains, from the bed, and turned down the sheet. 'I'll draw the curtains, too, shall I?' she said, straightening.

'No, please don't,' Leonie said, staring at the window and watching as sunlight shone through the clouds in the sky. The rain had stopped now; the clouds were blowing away. Leonie did not want to shut out the sun; it made her feel less bleak and depressed to see it.

'OK, then, have a nice rest,' said Marjorie cheerfully. The door closed behind her and Leonie was alone. She stood in the middle of the room, looking around, feeling lost and bewildered, and very much afraid.

This was her home now. She stared into the dressing-table mirror, her dark blue eyes enormous, incredulous. This wasn't happening, it couldn't be. She was not here, in Warlock House, Malcolm's home, as the wife of his brother.

Giles couldn't be her husband. He hated her, he always had; he had not wanted her to marry his brother, he had not wanted her to join his family. Yet she was here now, in this house, and she was his wife.

She put both of her cold, trembling hands to her face, her fingers exploring the delicate bones of her cheeks, temples, jaw. In the mirror the reflection did the same.

She still didn't believe it. She wished someone would tell her it was only a strange, terrifying dream, from which at any moment she would awake. None of this was real, including herself. She did not know that face she saw in the mirror, the face her fingers had touched. It couldn't be her, standing here, in this room; she did not know that girl with the huge, frightened eyes and white face, the strangely distorted body.

Turning away, she lay down on the bed and closed her eyes, but she couldn't sleep or even lie still; she kept twisting about, sighing. She couldn't stop thinking, yet her thoughts kept dissolving like wraiths vanishing into a mist; she had lost all sense of reality. She was like a leaf being carried helplessly on a strong flood towards ... what?

She turned over on to her side heavily, and her arm flew out and hit something which crashed to the floor with a noise like splintering glass. With a cry of shock, she sat up to see what she had knocked down.

As she did so, Giles strode into the room from his own. 'Are you OK?' he demanded harshly.

'I'm sorry, I've broken a glass!' she said, swinging her legs to the floor to stand up.

Giles grabbed her by the shoulders and pushed her back on to the bed, kneeling on it beside her, holding her down.

'Are you crazy? You could cut your foot open on that broken glass!'

She was trembling stupidly. 'I ... I didn't think ...'

'No, that's the trouble, you never do,' he muttered, staring down at her, and she looked back at him, her mouth dry. A strange confusion swept over her. She couldn't stop watching him, the strong face, the grey eyes which no longer looked cold, that mouth which had such passion in the hard, firm lines of it.

'The glass must be swept up before someone treads on it,' Giles said in a deep, husky voice.

'Yes,' she whispered. She must stop staring, stop thinking like this—what on earth was wrong with her? Her heart was beating heavily, fiercely, inside her, crashing against her ribs so hard that it made her almost sick.

Giles stared back at her, his skin flushed and taut, like her own. His eyes had a savage glitter, and she knew this time that it was not rage, it was the same primitive, physical reaction sweeping through her. He wanted her, in the same way she wanted him. He was staring at her mouth, and she felt her lips part and burn, and was terrified.

She drew an audible breath. 'We'd better call Marjorie!' she said loudly, and saw his eyes blink, his head snap back.

He let go of her and stood up beside the bed, avoiding the broken glass.

'Yes,' he said, in a rough, low voice, picked up the phone, and spoke into it, but she was so distraught that she didn't hear what he said.

He put the phone down, and said brusquely, 'She'll be up in a moment.' His mouth twisted in cold, sardonic mockery then, and he added, 'So you can stop shaking—you're quite safe!'

Turning on his heel, he walked out, and Leonie lay there, on the point of tears. Living in the same house as Giles was going to be like living on the edge of a volcano. How on earth was she going to survive it?

* * *

When she got up for lunch, though, Giles was politely distant, treating her like a visitor, almost a stranger. Leonie gratefully accepted his lead, talking small talk, avoiding all contact with him, trying never to meet his eyes.

When she went back to her room an hour later, he opened the door for her, a sardonic look in his face.

'Going to sleep for a while? Pleasant dreams.'

Leonie pretended not to hear any undertones in that comment, and stayed upstairs all afternoon. Dinner was a repeat of lunch: they talked politely and remotely and parted in the same way.

The pattern was set. Each day they had breakfast together, then went for a drive for an hour or two, exploring the countryside in that part of Essex. They returned in time for lunch, and then Giles insisted that she take a long rest on the bed in her room. At dusk they had drinks in the lounge before a light dinner, after which they listened to music or watched TV before Leonie went to bed early.

Giles treated her with cool courtesy and concern, and they talked quietly over meals, during their drives, in the evenings, getting to know each other a little better each day. He often surprised her; they had more in common than she had ever suspected—liked the same books, same music, same films. There was always something for them to talk easily about, at least. Sometimes, though, their eyes would meet and she would flush and look quickly away, but never before she had seen his mouth go crooked, and those cold grey eyes mock her.

He knew what he could do to her now, and she was disturbed by that expression in his eyes. She was glad she did not know what he was thinking. She knew now that he wanted her, but did he still bitterly resent having been forced to marry her? Did he still hate her?

By the end of that week, Leonie was almost eager to see Mrs Kent return. She was still nervous about her mother-in-law, but she hoped life would be a little easier if she was not always alone with Giles. He could then stop pretending that this was a real honeymoon, and go back to work, and perhaps she might feel less tense and edgy.

Mrs Kent arrived late on a cold, windy afternoon, complained of a headache after her long drive home, and went straight to bed.

In the morning, Giles left for the office early, before Leonie was up, and so Leonie faced her mother-in-law alone over breakfast.

Mrs Kent arrived after Leonie had eaten, paused in the doorway as though startled to see her, then muttered, 'Good morning,' and sat down opposite her at the table. She poured herself some orange juice, sipped it, took a slice of toast and spread a thin layer of marmalade on it in silence.

Leonie felt her spirits sink. Was this how it was to be? Grim silence? Hostility? Isolation? She did not know how she was going to stand it.

Then Mrs Kent looked up and gave her a quick look, frowning. 'Leonie...' she began, and then sighed, breaking off.

'Yes?' Leonie met her eyes, her own gaze pleading. She could not live in this house if both Giles and his mother were to be her enemies.

'Leonie,' Mrs Kent began again, then abruptly held out both her thin hands, which were trembling. 'My dear, don't look at me like that; you make me so ashamed... I wasn't kind to you; I wish I had been—you and Malcolm might have got married right away, and he wouldn't have gone skiing, and...' She broke off again, her lip quivering, her lashes wet with tears. 'Oh, but what's the use of wishing? You can't turn back the clock.' The tears began to trickle down her white cheeks.

'Please, don't...don't cry...' Leonie whispered, horrified, and Mrs Kent let go of her to run one hand over her own face, scrubbing away the tearstains.

'No, you're right—we mustn't cry over what we can't change,' she said in a husky voice. 'We have the future to think about. That is what matters now. The baby. His baby. When Giles told me, it was like a miracle—I'd been so unhappy, and then to hear that there was going to be a baby, Malcolm's baby. Oh, it changed everything. I've got something to live for again.' She pulled out a handkerchief and blew her nose, then managed a watery smile. 'If it is a boy, Leonie, you will call him Malcolm, won't you?'

'Yes, I mean to,' Leonie agreed, but she felt a shiver of odd uneasiness. Mrs Kent was an obsessive woman, and that made Leonie a little frightened.

What if Mrs Kent became too possessive over the baby? Tried to take it over completely? Leonie was not aggressive, her nature was too gentle for that, but if her mother-in-law became a threat she was determined that she would not back down. This was her baby, and she was not giving it up to anybody.

Two days later, she was taking a walk around the garden before lunch when she stopped with a gasp, her hand going to her back.

It couldn't be the baby coming! It wasn't due for ten days. The stabbing sensation subsided. She waited, gingerly massaging her back, but the pain seemed to have stopped. A false alarm? Slowly she began to walk back to the house, took off her coat and went to wash before lunch.

Another pain hit her as she turned on the taps. This time she was sure what it was, and, wincing, she looked at her watch. Well, it wasn't going to happen for a while, the pains were too far apart, but she had to face it: the baby was definitely on the way.

She decided not to say anything to her mother-in-law for the moment. She would eat her lunch first and wait until the pains were coming at much closer intervals. No point, yet, in alerting the maternity hospital in which she was going to have the baby. They would not want to see her until a much later stage.

Leonie had been afraid she would panic when the time came, but oddly enough she felt very calm and relaxed. She ate a light lunch of fruit and an omelette, then lay down on her bed, glad to be alone so that nobody should realise what was happening, and she could ride the pains without an audience. They were not very severe yet, and she found it helped to practise her breathing lessons.

It was four hours later that she finally decided it was time to admit she was in labour. Mrs Kent was the one who panicked. She began to shake, turning pale; could hardly dial the number of the hospital to warn them Leonie was on her way, and her voice broke as she called for George to drive Leonie there at once.

'I'm coming too!' she said, helping Leonie out of her chair. 'You'll want some support!'

The baby was born at nine o'clock that night, a boy weighing six pounds exactly, and it wasn't Mrs Kent who was there at the moment when Malcolm's son emerged into the world. In fact, she hadn't even been allowed to be present during labour. The ward sister firmly explained that only fathers were permitted to be present.

'This is my grandson!' Mrs Kent protested, scarlet with rage

'We don't know yet whether it is a boy or a girl, do we?' said the sister sharply. 'I'm sorry, but I cannot bend the rules for you or anybody else. Fathers only. This is a hospital, not a game show. I can't have my labour-room full of relatives!'

Mrs Kent looked as if she did not believe her ears, and Leonie had been horrified by the gathering storm, but she never knew what happened next because a nurse appeared at that moment and discreetly led her from the waiting-room into the labour ward.

So it was Giles who told Leonie she had a son. He arrived an hour after Leonie was wheeled into the labour-room, and was there throughout the birth, to her startled surprise. She had not expected it of him. It did not seem to be his scene.

When he first walked in, he looked so formal and elegant, wearing one of his dark grey pin-striped city suits, a cream silk shirt, and a dove-grey silk tie. He looked totally out of place, and she had stared at him almost angrily, her forehead beaded with sweat, her hair dishevelled, half inclined to ask him to go away, for heaven's sake, because she knew she looked terrible and she did not want him to see her looking this way.

'Are you the husband?' the midwife asked him, her eyes fascinated.

'Yes, what can I do to help?' Giles answered coolly, and then to Leonie's disbelief he took off his jacket and tight-fitting waistcoat, undid his tie and shed it, opened his shirt collar, rolled up his shirt-sleeves and took over from the busy young midwife, who was delivering another baby in a neighbouring cubicle.

Giles wiped her sweating face with a cool, moist sponge, talked soothingly to her in between the spasms of pain which came with each contraction, and when the pain began again helped her count down her breathing.

It was Giles who held her hand during the final stages, and Giles who said quietly at last, 'You have a son, Leonie, a wonderful little boy.'

She was lying there, exhausted by that final push and already on the dark verge of sleep, her eyes shut, but they opened at the sound of

Giles's voice, her lashes fluttering against her cheeks. She looked around the cubicle eagerly. 'A boy? Where is he? I want to see him.'

'You will later, but he's gone to the nursery for tonight,' the midwife said, and Leonie frowned, suddenly afraid.

'Why so soon? Why didn't you let me see him? Is there something wrong? Tell me——'

'He's perfect; there's nothing wrong at all,' Giles said quickly.

'Perfectly normal procedure,' said the midwife. 'You're tired and the baby is slightly premature, and we thought we would tuck him up in the nursery right away so that you could get some rest.'

'But I haven't even seen him!' protested Leonie. 'Bring him back.'

'Wait until you're in bed in the ward,' said the midwife calmly. 'Then we'll see.'

Giles bent down and said soothingly, 'I saw him, and, I promise you, he's fine; he has masses of hair, already jet black, and he's going to be tall, I think; his legs look very long—he's a real Kent.'

'Just like his father,' said the young midwife, smiling at Giles. He was the sort of father she liked to have at her births; he was capable and useful, he had taken a lot of her work off her hands, kept his wife happy and stable until the time when her own expertise was really needed.

Not to mention that he was very good to look at! Dark, like his son, she thought; tall and long-limbed, and had a charming smile when he wasn't too absorbed in his wife to turn it in the midwife's direction!

Leonie met Giles's eyes and read the mocking irony in them. The midwife was looking at him, but both of them thought of Malcolm. But he smiled at her, his cool mouth twisting.

'Yes,' he said. 'He is just like his father.'

CHAPTER SEVEN

A WEEK before Christmas that year, Leonie woke up early out of a very deep sleep and at once lifted her head, listening for some sound from Mal. He slept next door, in the old nursery, which had been redecorated while she was in hospital—a surprise present from Mrs Kent, whose passionate enchantment with her grandson needed expression.

Each time she had come to see them she had brought armfuls of toys and clothes for baby Malcolm, and flowers, magazines and books for Leonie. When they got back to Warlock House it was to find a uniformed nanny waiting in the nursery, which had been painted glossy white, then stencilled with animals in pastel shades— pink and blue and yellow and green.

Leonie had protested, 'I don't want him to have a nanny! I want to look after him myself!'

Earnestly, Mrs Kent had soothed, 'Of course you do, my dear, and of course you will, but babies are a twenty-four-hour responsibility, and, take my word for it, you'll be glad to have help with him. My children had a nanny. Nanny Grant—such a nice woman; she was with me for years, even after Malcolm grew up and went off to boarding-school. She had no family, you see. This was her only home by then. She was such a comfort to me after my husband died. We sat and talked for hours, about the children when they were small. She loved them, too—we shared them. I was very fond of her. I missed her when she died.'

'I remember Malcolm talking about her,' Leonie had admitted, and Mrs Kent had smiled a little mistily at her. Since the birth of her grandson she no longer seemed to be on the verge of tears every time anyone mentioned her dead son, but her love for Malcolm was as deep as ever.

'Well, my dear, Malcolm was the baby, the youngest, so she clung on to him longest.' Mrs Kent had sighed. 'I suppose she spoilt him. Well, we both did. But Nanny Grant really loved babies, and when I was interviewing girls to take care of Mal the thing I wanted to be sure about was that they loved babies.'

'This girl, Susan Brown, is highly trained,' Giles had intervened in a coldly remote voice. 'Whether she loves babies or not, she has been to a good training college, and she seemed very level-headed and sensible to me. You can trust her with the baby, Leonie—and, as to your not wanting a nanny, let me remind you, you were planning to leave him with someone else while you went back to work, so I don't see why you are making all this fuss.'

She had flushed angrily. 'I wanted to spend as much time as possible with him, too! I didn't intend to hand him over to a nanny all the time!'

'You're free to make whatever arrangements you wish with Susan Brown,' Giles had shrugged. 'She will want time off, you know; she won't be employed on a twenty-four-hour, seven days a week basis. I'm sure she will be only too happy to let you take care of the baby whenever you choose. I agreed that she should have weekends off, anyway, although she is ready to make a special arrangement should you need to go away at any time. It would only be a question of overtime. She will work a five-day week, in other words, and she would have free time during the day, plus some evenings off, but I've left it to you to make final arrangements with her about time off during the week.'

'It seems you've arranged everything!' Leonie had muttered crossly.

'You'll like her, my dear; she's a very nice girl,' Mrs Kent had coaxed. 'I'm quite sure you'll be pleased with her.'

Leonie had liked Susan, luckily; it would have been hard not to like her. Fresh-complexioned, with curly blonde hair and calm blue eyes,

Susan had a warm and friendly nature, and, above all, it was obvious from the start that she was enthralled with Mal. Leonie could not help liking someone who adored her baby.

They had talked over cups of coffee later that day and come to a very amicable and flexible agreement to share Mal, for the moment. Leonie would look after him in the mornings, Susan in the afternoons, and they would take it in turns to be on call during the evening and night. If Leonie wanted to go out in the morning, or Susan wanted to go out in the afternoon, that would be worked out between them.

'And when I start work we'll draw up a schedule acceptable to both of us,' Leonie had promised, and Susan had given her a surprised stare.

'Will you be going back to work, then?'

'Probably,' Leonie said defensively. 'But I'm not sure when, yet.'

'What sort of work do you do? Something exciting?'

'I was a secretary.'

'Oh,' said Susan, frowning. 'To someone important? Was it a highly paid job?' She was clearly baffled, especially when Leonie shook her head.

'It was nothing special, and I didn't earn that much, no.'

Susan pulled a face.

'Why are you looking at me like that?' Leonie asked, laughing.

Bluntly, Susan said, 'Well, if I was you, I'd much rather stay at home. I mean—you've got this marvellous house, and a lovely baby, and an absolutely terrific husband.'

Leonie flushed. 'I like my independence!'

She had a sneaking feeling Susan was right, though. It would be only too easy to forget about finding a job, settle down to enjoy the comforts of this luxurious home and the joy of her little boy.

But she couldn't get too accustomed to this life. One day she was going to have to leave. After all, her marriage was not a real one and might end at any time.

So she started reading the job advertisements in the local paper, getting some idea of the sort of work available. There were few good jobs on offer; this was a largely rural area. Any good office job meant a long drive to a nearby town.

There was some seasonal work as Christmas approached, but none of it was secretarial. Maybe in the New Year there would be more work around? she thought, turning over in bed, since she couldn't hear a sound from the nursery.

Mal was already living in a routine, waking, eating and sleeping regularly so that one could plan one's day more easily. Last night Susan had been to a party and had returned in the early hours, so she would be sleeping late, and Leonie was looking after Mal herself until midday, when Susan would take over.

She would get up in another five minutes and see to him, but first she stretched and yawned, her body warm and at ease under the covers.

She was wearing a gift Giles had given her while she was in hospital—a boxed set of exquisite nightwear, all matching: a nightdress, tiny bed-jacket, pyjamas and robe in pure silk, white, but with the monogram 'K' embroidered on them in black, and they had the simplicity of sheer elegance. They were designer-made, the label inside them carried a Paris name recognisable all over the world, and they must have cost a fortune.

He had handed the silver-wrapped box to her while one of the nurses watched, fascinated. Her hands rather shaky with surprise and nerves, Leonie had unwrapped the present, and stammered her thank-you, blushing.

'I look forward to seeing you wearing them,' Giles had drawled in that light, mocking tone which always made her so edgy with him.

The nurse watching them had giggled, but Leonie had kept her head down, pretending to admire the cut of the nightdress, but all the time fiercely aware of Giles watching her.

She had put the box away unopened when she had returned from the hospital, never intending to wear any of the contents, but the housekeeper, Marjorie, had come across the box and put all the lovely garments into a chest of drawers.

'They'll be ruined if you leave them in that box!' she had told Leonie, who had been glad Marjorie had not mentioned it in front of Giles.

Last night, coming to bed, she had found the nightdress laid out on her bed. She had stared down at it, grimacing. Marjorie strikes again! she had thought irritably, and had been inclined to put the nightdress away again, but that would have been to make it all seem too important, so she had worn it in bed last night.

A sudden sound made her jump and sit up again, the narrow straps of the nightdress sliding down over her shoulders, leaving them bare.

It was not Mal crying. It was someone opening her bedroom door.

She looked across the room, and through the half-light of the wintry dawn she saw Giles silhouetted in the doorway, and her nerves thudded in shock.

'Good, you're awake!' he said with what sounded to her like soft menace.

Leonie watched him in breathless suspension as he closed the door and began to walk towards her, his long, lean body shrouded in a black silk dressing-gown over matching pyjamas.

'What do you want?' she whispered, looking away from him because the way he was staring at her made her intensely conscious that her nightdress left most of her shoulders and breasts bare. She grabbed the sheet and pulled it up to hide herself.

He stopped beside the bed, and her eyes hurriedly flicked up to him in time to see his brows swooping upwards in mocking irony. 'It isn't so much what *I* want,' he drawled. 'Not just at the moment. It's what *he* wants...'

For a second she didn't understand. She had been so busy trying not to look at him that she had not seen that he was carrying the baby in his arms.

She went scarlet. 'Oh...yes, of course,' she stammered.

Why had she been such a fool? Now Giles knew that she had jumped to that wild conclusion, had had the crazy idea that he had come into her room to make some sort of pass at her, when all he was doing was bringing the baby to her. She wished the earth would open up and swallow her!

'I imagine he wants his breakfast,' Giles said in that cool, mocking voice.

'Yes, of course,' she said again huskily, wishing he would just hand Mal to her and go away. 'Did he wake you up? Sorry... I didn't hear him crying.'

'He wasn't yelling, just gurgling to himself, and chewing his fingers in a hungry way, but I must have been more wide awake than you are,' Giles said, then amazed her by adding, 'I changed his nappy in the nursery, and washed and changed him.'

'Oh,' she said, stunned. 'Oh, thank you, that... that's very kind.'

'I enjoyed looking after him,' Giles said gravely. 'Well, now all you have to do is feed him.'

On cue, Mal began to cry, screwing his little black head round to glare accusingly at her, and Giles laughed.

'And I don't think he's in a mood to wait much longer.'

To her horror, he promptly sat down on the side of her bed and handed Mal to her.

She looked down as the baby turned into her body, hunting for her nipple, nuzzling the smooth silk of her nightgown. At once, the milk began to rise, her breasts rounding, full and aching in readiness for that little mouth.

Giles watched her hesitate, and his mouth twisted ironically. 'I saw him at your breast the day he was born, remember?' he mocked, then, leaning over, he deftly undid the two buttons on the front of her nightdress.

Leonie was too shocked to move; she could scarcely breathe. His hand slid inside and she shuddered as she felt his fingers curl round her full breast, pushing back the silk still partially covering it.

She could hear him breathing audibly, thickly; he was staring down at her naked breast, face flushed, his grey eyes brilliant, the pupils glittering like jet, while his fingers were moving rhythmically, stroking the warm flesh, the hard nipple. Leonie closed her eyes, trembling, feeling deep inside her body a convulsive clutch of erotic excitement. It was so long since a man had touched her like that. She couldn't help the wild shiver of pleasure, the heat and ache of aroused desire between her thighs.

Then Mal began to cry again, louder this time, and the spell was broken. Leonie's eyes flew open, and she tensed, burning with shame.

Oh, God, what had she been about to do? What had he been about to do?

Giles laughed shortly, his hand falling from her breast. 'You'd better feed him before he screams the house down!' He got up and walked out so fast that she barely had time to realise he had gone before the door slammed. Like an automaton, Leonie put Mal to the breast, and felt him begin to suck hungrily.

She sat there while the baby fed, staring at nothing, stunned by a sudden realisation. She had wanted Giles badly just now; so badly that she was still shuddering with that need, but that was not what had shocked her.

I'm in love with him! she thought incredulously, and closed her eyes, a groan wrenched out of her. It couldn't be true! She had been ready to admit, for some time now, that she was attracted to him, even though her common sense told her it would be madness to let Giles suspect that, because he was more than capable of taking advantage of the way she felt, but love . . . no, she couldn't be in love with him!

It was too late, though, to tell herself that. From the instant that she first admitted her feelings, they began to grow, raging through her like a forest fire running out of control, devouring everything in its path.

How had it happened, though? When had it happened? How long had she felt like this? When had she stopped loving Malcolm and begun to feel like this about Giles?

She tried to conjure up Malcolm's face, to remember how much she had loved him. But Malcolm had been fading from her day by day for months now, withdrawing gently into a past which seemed ever more distant. It would soon be a year since he'd died, and she no longer felt the stab of pain or of passion. Malcolm was someone whose memory she would always cherish, he was the father of her child, but she no longer mourned bitterly for him. She had gradually stopped thinking about him; for her he had gone forever. There was a gulf between them now—she was on one side, alive, and Malcolm was on the other side of that abyss, and no longer in the same world as herself.

She would never forget him entirely, of course; she had loved him too much for that, but her love had become a gentle affection and her grief had become a quiet sadness, a resigned acceptance. She was alive, and she was a passionate woman; she needed an answering passion.

Oh, but from Giles, of all people? she thought, her face burning. Until this moment she had never felt an emotion she could not handle. She had never felt threatened by her own feelings, driven and torn in all directions. Her thoughts swirled like the dark centre of a maelstrom. She could not drag herself out of that chaos, back to safety.

She kept remembering the sensuality of his hands, the tormenting promise of his mouth, and she was dry-mouthed from the intensity of her own excitement.

She didn't want to admit it, but the truth kept forcing itself on her. If Mal hadn't been between them, if Mal hadn't begun to cry when he did, they would have made love.

Reminded of him, she looked down at his flushed face and dark head. He had finished feeding and was half asleep, head heavy against her arm.

She smiled involuntarily. He was so sweet when he was like this—sated, content, angelic.

She did up her nightdress with slow and careful fingers, so as not to disturb him, and lay back, keeping his small body in the crook of her arm, while she wondered how on earth she was going to face Giles after this.

He must know how close she had come to giving in to him, and he was an opportunist. She shuddered to think what he might be planning next. It had been understood between them that their marriage was not a real one; merely a legal fiction meant to ensure the Kent family's rights over her son. Giles needed not imagine that he had any rights over her, too!

It was another hour before she went downstairs, leaving baby Mal fast asleep in his swinging crib in the white-painted nursery. Leonie had dressed casually, in jeans and a fine blue cashmere sweater, her blonde hair tied up with blue ribbon and swinging in a pony-tail behind her head.

Giles was reading a newspaper over the breakfast table, although he had finished his breakfast. He was casually dressed, too, because this was a Sunday and he was not going to work. He wore a jade-green shirt, and over that a black sweater, with black denims, but managed to look as if dressed by a top French designer, which she suspected he might have been! His casual wear was often designer fashion; when he dressed for the City he wore classic, expensive English tailoring.

When she walked into the room he lowered the paper and studied her wryly, his brows lifting.

'You look about fifteen! Retreating into your teens, Leonie?' he drawled. 'It won't do you any good, you know. You can't escape from life; it has a nasty habit of catching up with you sooner or later.'

'You're being too clever for me!' she said coldly, sitting down at the table opposite him and pouring herself coffee.

He laughed. 'Oh, I think you know what I'm talking about. You'd like life to be as simple as ABC, wouldn't you? Malcolm was simple—he was glamorous and charming and he made you feel like a princess in a fairy-story. You're only happy thinking in stereotypes, so you cast me as the wicked brother because I was too blunt in saying that I didn't think you and Malcolm would be happy together. I was just the tyrant who was trying to stop your marriage to Malcolm, and you still see me the same way, don't you?'

She was not going to be dragged into a discussion on those lines, so she got up without answering him, without even giving him as much as a look, and made herself some toast in the electric toaster standing on the sideboard.

Still silent, she went back to the table, spread the toast with a thin layer of butter and marmalade and bit into it, although she was not at all hungry.

Watching her, Giles drily murmured, 'From your expression, I gather you're in a bad mood this morning! Feeling guilty, by any chance?'

She felt her cheeks burn. 'I have nothing to feel guilty about!'

He laughed. 'Oh, I agree—but you don't, do you? You're still trying to stay faithful to Malcolm's memory, but this morning in your bedroom you forgot all about him for a minute——'

'Shut up!' She got up, very flushed and angry, her chair falling over. 'I'm not staying here to listen to this!'

Giles got to his feet, too, flinging down his paper. 'Oh, sit down again and eat your breakfast. I'm going—you can stop trembling and looking so stricken.'

He walked to the door and she slowly sat down again, her hand shaking as she reached for her coffee-cup. Giles paused, glancing over his shoulder, his face impassive once more.

'Oh, by the way, we're going to a Christmas party tonight, given by my godfather, Lord Cairnmore. It won't be a large party, but everyone there will know me, so I want you to make a good impression. Wear something special.'

She resented the peremptory tone.

'Don't you give me orders!' she threw back at him, glaring across the room. 'I'm not one of your possessions, or a servant—and I'm not dressing to please you, or impress your friends! I'm not going to this party with you.'

He turned glittering eyes on her. 'You will go!'

Her dark blue eyes were spitting fire. 'You can't make me!'

'Can't I?' He laughed and his tone was light, but it was still a challenge and she faced it, her chin up, very flushed and defiant. He wasn't taking her seriously, and it was time he did.

'No, you can't!'

'Do you want to bet?' he mocked.

'I mean it, Giles!' she said angrily.

'And so do I,' he said through his teeth. 'Now, stop being silly, Leonie. This party is being given for us. My godfather wants to meet you, he wants to introduce you to our friends. Our wedding was very private, none of them were invited; they're curious. Good heavens,

Leonie—every one of them will expect my wife to be there!'

'Stop calling me your wife!' she muttered, wildness in her veins. She knew she was provoking another scene and it was folly, but she couldn't stop.

'That's what you are!' Giles snarled as his temper flared higher. 'You're my wife. My *wife*, Leonie! Start believing it, because it's a fact!'

His face was darkening with anger, and she was glad. She hoped he would lose his temper. Why should he stay in control of himself when she had lost all command of herself and her emotions?

He took a long, threatening stride back towards her, and she leapt to her feet again and faced him, bristling.

'I'm not really your wife, this isn't a real marriage, it's just a legal fiction for Mal's sake.'

'Never mind Mal—leave him out of this,' Giles said curtly.

'How can I? He's the only reason I let you talk me into that phoney wedding, and why you insisted on marrying me, too!'

'Oh, there were other reasons, believe me, Leonie!' he said mockingly, and was suddenly too close for comfort, his grey eyes glittering down at her.

'What other reasons?' she whispered breathlessly, and then could have bitten her tongue out. How could she have been such a fool as to ask that? This was a game Giles Kent had played often in the past, but she was a clumsy newcomer to sophistication; he was running rings around her.

His smile taunted, gleaming with amusement. 'Do you want me to show you again? Come back upstairs and I'll be glad to.'

She slapped his face as hard as she could, and felt him rock on his heels in shock. He looked at her in icy fury, mouth tight, a white line around it, jaw set, eyes violent.

'Don't ever strike me again, Leonie. Next time, I might hit you back!'

'That would be better than having you kiss me!' she flung at him, and saw the rage in his face with a sense of reckless satisfaction in having got under his skin. He wasn't quite so cool now!

For a moment she didn't know what he would do next—he looked so angry that she felt her heart beating in her very throat—but then they both heard Marjorie coming towards the door, her footsteps echoing on the wood-block flooring in the hall.

Giles glanced at the door and stiffened, a cold mask coming down over his face again. 'Listen,' he said harshly, 'you had better be ready for this party tonight, or I will personally come up to your room and dress you, and then carry you downstairs over my shoulder if I have to! And don't think I don't mean it. Because, I assure you, I do. You are my wife and not in name only. If you want to force a showdown between us that's up to you, but, I promise you, you won't enjoy what happens.'

CHAPTER EIGHT

ALL that day Leonie swung between one mood and another: one moment determined to defy him, the next deciding that discretion might be the better part of valour. She stayed close to her mother-in-law as much as she could to keep Giles at bay, but it did not stop him watching her, those grey eyes of his gleaming with mockery and warning. He had meant it, she could be sure of that.

At half-past six, after they had all watched the TV news, he glanced at his watch and got up. 'Time to take a shower and get dressed for the party, Leonie,' he drawled.

His mother smiled, her fingers busily knitting a sweater for the baby. 'Of course, I'd forgotten Cairnmore's party. I'm sure you'll enjoy that, Leonie. He's such a kind man.'

'Are you coming?' Leonie asked hopefully, but her mother-in-law shook her head.

'No, my dear, I was invited, but I'd rather have an early night.'

'Come along, Leonie,' Giles murmured, his fingers curling round her arm and fastening into an iron bracelet.

She couldn't struggle, not in front of his mother. She had to let him steer her out of the room, but when the door shut behind them and they were at the foot of the stairs she tugged free, glaring.

'Don't manhandle me!'

'I wouldn't need to if you didn't keep arguing!'

Marjorie appeared, carrying a tray towards the dining-room to lay the dinner table for Mrs Kent. She gave them a puzzled, surprised look. Leonie forced a stiff smile, and walked up the stairs with Giles behind her. She couldn't fight him with Marjorie watching them.

Hurrying into her bedroom a moment later, she quickly slammed the door and tried to lock it, but the key had gone.

She stood, staring, and heard Giles on the other side of the door, his voice amused. 'I'll come and find you when I'm ready—you've got about half an hour, Leonie!'

He walked on along the corridor, and she backed, forehead corrugated, wondering what to do—should she give in, or refuse to go to this party?

How dared he remove the key from her bedroom door? How dared he threaten her? Who did he think he was?

She heard his shower running, and looked at her watch. Time was rushing past; she had to make up her mind.

But she knew she had. She was too scared of a scene in this house, with her mother-in-law and the servants listening. Giles knew that, damn him.

She threw open her wardrobe and looked at her clothes. What was she going to wear? She didn't have many clothes which were suitable for a smart party. All the women there tonight were going to be dressed to kill.

Then her eye fell on one dress she had not worn for many months. She couldn't have got into it while she was pregnant. Malcolm had chosen it, picked it out for her to wear at a party they had gone to just over a year ago. She had felt very self-conscious in it, and had only worn it that once, although it had made quite a stir at the party. But it had been Malcolm's favourite dress and he had constantly urged her to wear it, without success. A sexy black satin, it was skin-tight, hugging her body from her breasts down to her knees but leaving much of the rest of her bare: her arms, her shoulders, her throat and the beginning of her breasts. She knew it made men stare, but she had never been the sort of girl who enjoyed that sort of attention.

An angry little smile curled her lips. Giles wanted her to 'impress' his friends, did he?

She pulled out the black dress and held it up against herself, staring at her reflection in the long mirror in the wardrobe door, then she laid the dress over her bed and went to have a shower.

Giles opened her door some half an hour later and stopped in his tracks, his eyes narrowing and his jawline tight.

She pretended to ignore him, her attention given to a wayward strand of blonde hair which kept trying to curl the wrong way, but of course she was tensely waiting for his reaction to the way she looked.

Curtly, he suddenly snapped, 'Oh, no!'

'What?' Leonie asked, all innocence.

'I'm not taking you, looking like that!' he grated, and she swung to face him, blue eyes wide and mock-surprised.

'What do you mean?'

'You know perfectly well what I mean,' Giles said through his teeth.

'Don't you like the way I look?' she murmured, smoothing a hand down over the clinging black satin.

His eyes followed the movement of her hand, down over her swelling breasts, the small waist and rounded hips, and she heard the intake of his breath, saw the flare of his nostrils, the glitter of those hard grey eyes. 'Be careful, or I'll show you just how much!' he muttered thickly, and suddenly Leonie couldn't breathe.

Giles watched the colour creep up her face, and he laughed. 'And there isn't time for that!'

Leonie couldn't think of any answer for that, but he didn't wait for her to answer him, anyway; he looked at his watch, and grimaced. 'There isn't time for you to change into something more suitable, either!'

'You told me to put on my best dress!' she snapped. 'Well, this is it! It was Malcolm's favourite, anyway.'

A long silence followed, charged with an intensity she felt in every nerve of her body, then Giles swung on his heel and walked out, saying over his shoulder, 'We're going to be late if we don't hurry.'

She picked up her short evening coat, a quilted black velvet lined with silk, slid into it, collected her matching black velvet evening bag, and followed him more slowly, getting cold feet now that she was on her way to the party.

His wealthy, snobbish friends were going to stare at her in disbelief, their respectability outraged by the very sight of her. She felt her heart sink. Why had she done it? Oh, she had told herself she was putting on the black dress to annoy Giles, but that hadn't been true.

She knew she had been kidding herself. The truth was, she had wanted to see that look on his face; it excited her to excite him, and that was stupid, that was crazy, because it was dangerous.

She was in his power. Wasn't that bad enough? Why had she put ideas into his head by dressing this way tonight? She had never liked living dangerously, she wasn't the sort of girl who enjoyed walking a tightrope, and the last thing in the world she wanted was to attract Giles. Wasn't it?

She bit her lip, shivering. Well, wasn't it? she asked herself angrily, and the question echoed inside her head without any answer coming back.

What *is* the matter with me? she thought. What is going on? She looked down the stairs to where Giles waited for her, a tall man, his face hard, his body lean and powerful in his formal black evening suit, and felt almost sick with nerves and a strange yearning.

Oh, no, she thought: I'm not really falling in love with him, am I? That really would be insanity. I can't let it happen.

She almost turned and fled back up to the safety of her room, but at that instant Mrs Kent came out to say goodbye to them, her eyes wid-

ening at the sight of Leonie in the very provoc-
ative dress.

Heaven knew what she thought, but she
didn't make any comment, just said, 'Have a
lovely evening, both of you!'

Leonie managed a shy smile before Giles took
her by the arm and steered her out of the house
into the waiting car. George was driving them,
so that Giles could drink at the party. With another pair of ears attentive to everything they
said, they were almost silent during the drive,
which only lasted ten minutes, anyway.

There was a line of cars turning into the great
wrought-iron gates leading into the park around
Cairn House. George slotted into place at the
end of the procession, and they made their way
at a funereal pace, their wheels grating on the
gravelled drive. Looking out of the windows,
Leonie saw little of the parkland; a dim outline
of a tree here, the white blur of a grazing sheep
there.

'What time shall I pick you up, sir?' asked
George as he opened the car door for them in
front of the elegant portico of the large white
eighteenth-century house, which was one of the
loveliest stately homes in Essex.

'Eleven-thirty, unless I ring to change the
time,' Giles said.

Leonie was staring up at Cairn House, which
was floodlit, giving something of the effect of

moonlight on the perfectly proportioned façade of the building. She had seen it from the road as she'd driven past, but she had never been able to see it close up, and, of course, she had never been inside. It was wonderful, she thought, transfixed. She had always thought Warlock House was beautiful, but this was in another league altogether. It was a work of art.

George drove on, and Giles and Leonie turned towards the steps leading up to the portico, under which waited Lord Cairnmore himself, a grizzled, upright figure in evening dress, his silver hair gleaming in the darkness.

Giles put a hand under her elbow and led her up to meet his godfather, who smiled down at her with a mixture of curiosity and admiration.

'This is Leonie, sir,' Giles said, and the old man held out his hand.

'Leonie. I am very pleased to meet you at last. I wish I could have been at your wedding, but unluckily I was abroad. I hope you and Giles are going to be very happy, my dear.'

She murmured, 'Thank you,' shyly, and he smiled again.

'You know, this is a very elusive fox you've managed to corner! A lot of pretty girls have hunted him in the past without success, and everyone was incredulous when they heard that he was getting married at last—but one look at you makes it very clear why you pulled it off where they failed! Every man here tonight is going to envy him. I do myself! Giles, I hope you know what a lucky fellow you are?'

'I do indeed,' Giles drawled.

Leonie liked Lord Cairnmore; there were lines of humour and kindliness in his face, but there was strength there, too.

'I hope I'm going to see a lot of you in the future, Leonie,' he said, and she smiled up at him, surprised and relieved that he was being so welcoming. She had not expected this warmth.

'Thank you, Lord Cairnmore.'

'Call me Harry,' he said.

'Stop flirting with my wife, sir!' Giles said, looking wryly amused.

'Was I?' The older man pretended surprise, then grinned at him. 'Sorry about that, Giles! But that's something you are going to have to get used to, I'm afraid. You shouldn't have married someone this gorgeous if you didn't want other men to look at her!'

'Looking is OK,' Giles drawled, sliding his arm around Leonie's waist in a proprietorial, possessive gesture. 'So long as they don't go any further than that!'

Lord Cairnmore laughed loudly. 'Going to be a jealous husband, are you, Giles? Well, why not? Why not? Don't blame you. Take her inside and get her a drink. I'll see you later.'

He turned to welcome some new arrivals, and Leonie and Giles moved on into the candlelit hall, fragrant with bowls and great vases of flowers, where they were welcomed by Lord Cairnmore's elder daughter, Jess Cutler, whose husband, Neil Cutler, was a famous polo player and horse breeder.

Leonie had seen photos of Jess Cutler in the Press often enough to recognise her at sight. A woman of around forty, Mrs Cutler was herself reputed to be one of the best riders in England, and she certainly had a face like a horse, a well-bred horse, with a long, thin nose and high forehead, straight brown mane and enormous, staring eyes.

After shaking hands with Leonie, to whom she said very little, she talked to Giles about mutual friends, braying with laughter now and then.

Suddenly, she said, 'Can't believe it, you know. You, of all people, getting married! I tell you, Neil almost burst into tears. He thinks it is a terrible waste, he says. He did say he was going to ask you to let him have your little black book, so that he could console all your old flames, but, if he asks you, you had better not say yes, or I'll be after you!'

Giles laughed. 'Don't worry, I won't let him have it!'

'I should hope not,' she said in her loud, assured, arrogant voice, then glanced at Leonie before saying, 'Which reminds me, I'd better warn you: Steff is here.'

Leonie stiffened, her face going blank, masklike, while behind that her mind was busy working out what Mrs Cutler meant.

Steff? Who was Steff? Then it dawned—Mrs Cutler must mean Stephanie Ibbotson, a vivacious redhead Giles had been dating around the time Malcolm first took Leonie home to meet his family.

Stephanie Ibbotson might be designing gardens for wealthy clients at the moment, but she had been a photographer at one time, and had once been a photographic model herself, when she was about eighteen. She had never quite hit the heights in any of her careers, but she did have a genius for self-publicity, which meant that she was well known in spite of not being a huge success.

'I didn't know she was a friend of yours, Jess,' Giles drawled, his expression bland. If the news that Stephanie Ibbotson was here worried him, he certainly did not show it by so much as a flicker.

'I wouldn't call her a friend,' Jess Cutler said with faint hauteur. 'She's designing a garden for me. You know Neil inherited a manor house over the border in Suffolk from a cousin last year? Place hadn't been touched for years; garden gone to seed, house worse. We had to wait all this time to get possession—you know how the lawyers drag their feet on these things. Anyway, we couldn't possibly move in, of course, not with the place the way it was, so I got a good architect and builder to do the house, and Steff to do the garden for me.'

'She's very talented,' Giles murmured, and Leonie shot him a glance.

In what direction? she wondered acidly, and then caught his eye and hurriedly looked away, hoping he had not read her expression. She did not want him to think she was jealous. She wasn't, of course. Not in the least.

'Oh, she's doing a wonderful job! Transforming the place! Of course, gardens take time, but already you can see it's going to be absolutely fabulous.' Jess looked past Giles into a panelled reception hall behind him. 'And speak of the devil, there she is!'

Leonie and Giles followed her glance, both of them immediately recognising the young man talking to Stephanie Ibbotson.

'I told her to bring someone and she turned up with a good-looking young doctor,' said Jess, laughing. 'It gives a whole new meaning to the words private medicine, doesn't it?'

Neither of them laughed, but Jess was oblivious to their stiff expressions. Her eyes flicked

past them and her face lit up. 'Gerry, darling—
wonderful that you could come!'

She darted off to greet the newcomer with
outstretched hands. It was no surprise that he
should be another of the horsy fraternity; a
bluff man in his thirties with a fresh complex-
ion, hard face and casual manner.

Giles said coldly, 'The guy with Steff is the
fellow who came to the wedding, isn't it?
Andrew something or other. The one who offered you a flat?'

Leonie nodded, frowning. 'I can't understand what *he* is doing here!' she thought aloud.

'Did you expect him to stay faithful to you
forever?' Giles asked with a sting in his voice,
and she flushed.

'Andrew was never involved with me—it was
Angela he was seeing!'

Giles looked at her sharply, frowning.
'Angela?'

'Yes.' Leonie was feeling guilty because she
had forgotten all about Angela since the birth of
baby Malcolm. So much had happened, she had
had so much on her mind. 'I should have rung
or written,' she said regretfully. 'She came to see
me and Mal while I was in hospital, but since
then I haven't seen her. I kept meaning to get in
touch with her, but there was always so much to
do. Maybe she and Andrew have split up? I do

hope not; he's so nice, and Angela was really serious about him.'

'From the way Steff is gazing up at him, I'd hazard a guess that she's pretty serious about him, too,' Giles said with a sort of venom, and Leonie wondered if he was jealous. Which of them had ended their relationship—Giles or Stephanie Ibbotson? How did he really feel about her? Leonie's heart sank as she stared across the room at the other girl. Stephanie Ibbotson was beautiful, so vibrant with that red hair and vivid green eyes, her figure dynamic and sexy in a jade-green silk dress. She made Leonie feel colourless and boring.

'That seems to bother you,' Giles said in a clipped way.

Starting, Leonie looked up at him, stammering. 'What? No...I...why should it? I just didn't think Andrew was the type to switch girlfriends every few weeks.'

Giles bit out irritably, 'You don't know who broke it off—him or your friend Angela. She has had quite a few men in her life, hasn't she? She isn't the faithful type, exactly.'

Frowning, Leonie said, 'You don't know her well enough to say something like that!'

'Malcolm talked about her a couple of times. I got a pretty clear idea of what she was like.'

'Angela has been unlucky with her men,' Leonie muttered. 'She always seems to pick the wrong ones.'

'That's a classic pattern with men and women,' Giles said, drily, and she wasn't sure exactly what he meant by that. There was something in his expression that made her feel he was not just talking about Angela. He had always made it plain that he thought she was the wrong girl for Malcolm—was he obliquely saying so, again?

She met his eyes angrily, reacting more to what she thought he might be hinting at than to what he had actually said. 'Why are you always so censorious? What makes you an expert on the subject? And don't say anything against Angela—she's my best friend, I've known her since we were at school together!'

Giles laughed suddenly, his face relaxing. 'Oh, I'm up against the freemasonry of women, am I? Oh, well, I won't say another word. Angela is perfect, of course.'

Leonie bit her lip, then laughed, too.

They stood there, smiling at each other; and Leonie felt a strange happiness flooding through her; she felt weightless, as if she could float, and as free as a bird. She could almost believe that if she tried she would be able to fly. She could not ever remember being this happy for a very long time, and that was amazing, that was incredible, because it meant that Giles had made her happy simply by smiling at her, and that might be frightening if she let herself dwell on it. Was he becoming that important to her?

'Leonie?' a startled voice said beside them a moment later, and with a wrench she tore her eyes away from Giles and turned to look at the other man who had come up to them.

'Oh . . . Andrew . . .' she stammered, her voice husky and unsteady because she was still reverberating with the wild happiness she had felt when Giles had smiled at her.

'I can't believe my eyes!' Andrew said, gazing at the way the skin-tight black satin dress followed every curve of her body. He grinned wryly. 'Sorry if I'm staring, but the last time I saw you you looked so different.'

'I was seven months pregnant at the time!' she said lightly.

'So you were!' Andrew laughed, then caught sight of the black scowl Giles wore, and stopped smiling. 'Congratulations on your son,' he said quickly, changing the subject. 'I heard all about him from Angela.'

Leonie gave him an uncertain glance, wondering whether or not to ask the obvious question. 'How is she? I haven't seen her for ages.'

'Neither have I,' Andrew said, grimacing. 'She got a job working with some film crew, making costumes, and went off to Spain for three months to work out there. I had a few postcards and phone calls at first, then nothing, so I don't know if I'll ever see her again.'

Leonie impulsively took his hand, squeezing it warmly. 'I'm sorry, Andrew. Angela has always... well...' She didn't know quite how to phrase it, but Andrew grimaced and bluntly said it for her.

'She's fickle, you mean? Yes, I've realised that now. I did think we had something special, and I was knocked for six for a few weeks, but I'm getting over it now. I've met this terrific girl...' He grinned, and Leonie laughed.

'Oh, I am glad,' she said, and he put an arm around her, hugging her in a brotherly way.

'You're so sweet, Leonie!'

There was a rustle of silk next to them a second later, and then Stephanie Ibbotson drawled, 'Giles, what *is* going on here? Are you going to let every man in the place make love to your wife?'

'You think I should knock your new boyfriend down?' Giles enquired blandly.

Stephanie laughed, looking far from amused. 'Darling, how primitive and thrilling—I believe you would!'

'And you're right,' he said through tight lips.

Stephanie ran a hand up and down his arm, feeling his muscles. 'I do love dangerous men!'

she cooed, and Leonie's teeth met. She did not like Stephanie Ibbotson.

'No,' Stephanie said, sounding reluctant. 'No, don't spoil the party, Giles. I'm sure Andrew is going to be a good boy now, aren't you, Andrew, darling?'

Andrew gave her a faintly uncertain smile. He was not the ultra-sophisticated type and wasn't sure how to take her idea of a joke.

'Oh, come on, Steff! You don't really think I was making a pass at Leonie?' he muttered, darkly flushed. 'Honestly!'

'Well, what's sauce for the goose is certainly allowed to the gander,' Stephanie said with a smouldering look, put her arms around Giles's neck, swayed closer until their bodies touched, and kissed him on the mouth, lingeringly.

His hand automatically came up to grip her waist, and Leonie felt a stab of pain so sharp and fierce that it took her breath away. Shaken, she thought, I'm a fool; he's the last man to fall in love with, and it is crazy to feel this jealousy because he doesn't care a jot for me, he only married me to keep control of his brother's child, his brother's share of the family estate. I must not love him.

But how did you stop? To say 'stop' to love was like trying to float instead of falling after you had jumped out of an aeroplane without a parachute. You might be able to manage that for a little while, but sooner or later gravity triumphed and you plummeted, like Icarus, falling out of a blue sky after flying too high.

'Behave yourself, Steff!' Giles drawled, and Leonie reluctantly looked back to see him holding Stephanie at arm's length, his hands grasping her shoulders.

Stephanie looked at him through half-closed, flirtatious, cat-like eyes, and Leonie watched bleakly, hating her.

'Darling, you're still the sexiest man I know!' the other woman purred, her red mouth curving in feline satisfaction, the cat after it had swallowed the cream.

Andrew had stiffened and was pale. Frowning, he turned away and walked off. Steff looked after him, her mouth quirking.

'Oh, dear, someone is sulking!'

There was a smear of that vivid lipstick on Giles's mouth. Leonie looked at it with distaste. Giles met her eyes, no doubt read her expression, and pushed Stephanie away. Pulling out a handkerchief, he wiped his mouth, but she knew she would not so easily be able to erase the memory of seeing Stephanie in his arms. Oh, she had always known that he had had affairs; Malcolm had laughingly almost boasted about it. He was quite proud of his elder brother's success with women. But now Leonie had seen him with one of his women, and it hurt.

'You had better go after your new plaything if you don't want someone else to grab him,' Giles said to Steff, and Leonie wondered if it hurt him to see her with Andrew, with any other man.

How did he really feel about Steff? Pain twisted inside her like a dagger, and she had to close her lips tightly to stop a cry of agony escaping.

'He's very cute,' Stephanie said with a wry smile. 'See you later, Giles; have fun.'

She ignored Leonie and walked away. Giles gave Leonie a searching stare.

'Still in a bad mood? Well, come and meet some of my friends, and try to be polite, and smile, for heaven's sake!'

She didn't argue—she was too busy fighting with the pain in her chest. Obediently, she followed him, a fixed smile on her pale face, hoping he would not notice her misery.

The rest of the party seemed to pass in a strange dream-like fashion; she talked to people without really knowing what she was saying or who they were, sipped champagne, nibbled desultorily at the elegant food from the buffet table, although she did not really want any, and throughout it all felt totally unreal.

Giles introduced her to a string of his friends, and she liked a number of them very much. Some were polite, some warm and friendly, others, though, were neither, and she didn't miss the curiosity in people's faces when they talked to her.

Everyone knew, of course, that she and Giles had got married just weeks before she'd had a baby, and it was obvious that guests at the party were whispering about it in every corner. She was conscious of being watched, edgily aware of scandalised or fascinated stares, of a mixture of disapproval, dislike and envy.

She coped with all that by withdrawing behind a wall; pretending not to care or even be aware of those reactions, just smiled and made small talk without allowing anyone to really reach her. She hoped she was convincing most of them, but knew she had not fooled Giles, who kept giving her a piercing stare, frowning.

She had not fooled Andrew, either, it seemed. 'You don't look happy,' he said some time during the evening.

'Don't I?' She laughed with a tang of bitterness, wishing he were not so sharp-eyed. 'Well, I've had a difficult year, I suppose.'

'I know you have, Leonie,' Andrew said gently. 'It must have been an enormous strain, coping with everything that's happened. I only hope this marriage of yours isn't going to make things worse.'

'Angela talks too much!' she said with a grimace.

He laughed. 'Doesn't she, though? I'm sorry if you mind my knowing.'

He had a sympathetic face, a lovely smile. 'No, I don't really mind,' Leonie said, smiling back. 'And there are good things to balance out the bad; I've got a lovely baby, and I'm healthy—what more can I ask?'

'If there is ever anything I can do...' Andrew offered, and she gave him a grateful look.

'Thank you, you're very kind, Andrew.'

At that moment, Giles came up to them and said curtly, 'We ought to be on our way. Didn't you say you wanted to get back to feed the baby?'

'Is he still on night feeds?' asked Andrew with professional interest, and Leonie smilingly shook her head.

'Mostly he sleeps right through to the six o'clock morning feed, but sometimes he's hungrier than usual, and wakes up during the night. That happens less and less often, though, thank heavens. I can usually count on an unbroken night's sleep.'

'He sounds like the perfect baby,' Andrew said with amusement. 'I must meet this paragon!'

'Next time you're driving down to visit your mother, drop in and see us!' Leonie impulsively invited.

'Are we leaving now or not?' Giles bit out before Andrew could answer that. He caught her arm and began to walk away, pulling her with him without giving her time to say goodnight to Andrew.

He only paused *en route* for the front door to say a few words to his godfather. 'Wonderful party—we had a great time. Afraid we must leave now, our car will be waiting outside. Thank you for inviting us.'

'Glad you enjoyed yourself, my boy,' Lord Cairnmore said with something like irony. 'I wasn't sure you had.' Giles scowled, and his godfather grinned, then said, 'Leonie, a pleasure to meet you, and I shall be over soon to look at the latest addition to the Kent family.'

She smiled warmly at him. 'I'll look forward to seeing you, Lord Cairnmore.'

'Harry,' he reminded, leaning down to kiss her on the cheek.

'Goodnight, sir,' Giles said in that sharp, curt voice, jerking her away and striding out of the house. The winter night was cold. There was no cloud cover, the stars were fixed and bright overhead, but Leonie had no time to look up and admire them. George was waiting; they got into the car and a moment later were driving back to Warlock House.

She sat staring out of the window. Giles looked at her as if he hated her—and she was crazy about him. Why was life such hell?

CHAPTER NINE

MRS KENT was in bed by the time they got back to Warlock House, and most of the rooms were dark. Leonie turned at once towards the stairs, saying over her shoulder as she began to climb them, 'I'm tired—I'll check on Mal, and if he's asleep I'll go straight to bed, I think.'

Giles didn't answer; he strode into the sitting-room, where a faint amber light glowed from one of the table lamps. She faintly heard the chink of a decanter, then the sound of something being poured into a glass. Hadn't he had enough to drink at the party? Not that he seemed to be drunk, but she already knew him well enough to realise that he had a hard head and could drink quite a lot without showing it.

Leonie paused outside the nursery door, listening. She had left Susan in charge of baby Malcolm, but there was no sign of her. She slept in a room on the other side of the nursery, but after being up so late the night before Susan was probably fast asleep, and might well have slept through any crying from the baby.

Softly opening the door, Leonie tiptoed in and listened before approaching the swinging cradle in which baby Malcolm slept. She did not put on the light, but she could see quite well by the light from the corridor outside. He was curled round, one tiny hand flung out, palm upward, his face flushed with sleep, his breathing almost silent. Leonie was tempted to bend down and kiss him, but that would wake him, so after a moment she crept out again and closed the door without making a sound. With any luck he might sleep until morning.

In her own room, she kicked off her high heels and yawned, realising only then how sleepy she was, stretched and reached for the zip on the skin-tight black dress. Getting out of it was almost as tough as getting into it! You needed to be something of a contortionist.

She hadn't been able to lock her door because Giles still had the key, but before she got into bed she would put a chair under the handle to make sure the door could not be opened from the outside. Not that she was afraid of him! She had lived here for some months now, and Giles had never once tried to come into this room.

The zip slid down, she peeled the dress off and carefully hung it up in her wardrobe, then sat down on the edge of her bed to take off her stockings. She was wearing a black silk French basque corselet which pushed up her breasts and pulled in her small waist even further, giving her an hourglass figure. It ended above the thigh with a flurry of richly decorated black lace, very sexy against her white skin.

Her stockings were black, too, very sheer and fine. She didn't get time to take them off. The door opened and Giles walked in while she was sitting there, one knee lifted so that she could unhook her suspenders.

Giles didn't say anything, he just stood there, staring, and her heart beat so heavily that she almost thought she was going to faint.

'Get out of my room!' she whispered.

'So *this* is what was under that sexy black dress!' he merely said.

'Get out!' she said again, trying to sound angry but afraid she sounded more scared.

'I've been wondering all evening,' was all he said, looming over her in a way that made her even more nervous. 'I'd bet a lot of other men have been, too. I saw them watching you, their eyes popping out of their heads, every damn one of them imagining what was underneath that dress.'

She couldn't shout at him, for fear of waking baby Mal. Very flushed, she muttered furiously, 'That's enough! Go away.'

'Not yet,' he drawled. 'Not before we've had a talk.'

'At this hour?' She didn't know what he was doing in here, why he was tormenting her like this, but she was trying not to look as worried as she felt in case it made him more dangerous. 'It's very late, after all,' she said in a tone she forced to sound polite. 'Whatever you want to say can wait.'

'No, it can't,' he bit out.

'Look,' she snapped back, 'I was getting ready for bed.'

'So I see,' he drawled, and his grey eyes wandered over her barely clothed figure with a mocking insolence that made her want to hit him. How dared he look at her like that?

'And we've got nothing to talk about!' she defiantly threw at him.

'You know that isn't true, Leonie,' Giles murmured, and then to her shock and disbelief he knelt down in front of her.

She looked down at him, her dark blue eyes enormous, their pupils dilated and as black as jet.

'Here I am, at your feet,' Giles said with light mockery, and then, while she was still off balance from that remark, his hand lifted to touch her thigh.

Leonie gave an audible intake of breath, stiffening. 'What do you think you're doing?'

'You can see what I'm doing.' Giles slowly began to undo her suspenders, his fingers cool as they brushed against her skin. A shudder of aroused excitement went through her, although she could have kicked herself for responding like that.

'Stop that!' she whispered to cover how she really felt.

He gave her a glinting look from under his lashes, his mouth wickedly amused. 'You want them off, don't you? Weren't you taking them off when I arrived?' He was peeling one stocking down now, taking his time, and she was beginning to tremble violently.

'But I prefer to do it myself!'

He laughed mockingly. 'Ah, but I'll enjoy doing it far more!'

Her skin burned; she couldn't think of anything to say, and while she was trying to pull herself together Giles was deftly busy.

One stocking was completely off, and he began to remove the other one, his fingertips sending a shudder through her as they touched her inner thigh in intimate contact.

'You have terrific legs,' he said, staring down at them. 'Nice slim ankles, pretty feet, and such smooth skin.'

The other stocking was off, her legs were bare, and he was stroking them, from thigh to calf, sending shivers down her spine. She pulled her foot out of his hand and stood up, not knowing quite how to get him to leave.

He got to his feet, too, and, before she could get away, caught hold of her bare shoulders, forcing her round to face him, their bodies almost touching.

He was still in his evening suit; the grave formality made him look even taller, and was in strange contrast to her own half-naked informality, in the black basque. It was like a scene from some impressionist painting; sensuous, suggestive. Leonie found it disturbing, yet exciting, too, and that bothered her even more.

'Let go of me!' she protested, struggling.

'Not until we've had that talk!'

'We can talk tomorrow.'

'I've waited long enough as it is,' Giles said angrily, his face tightening. 'And tonight I realised I couldn't afford to wait any longer, or it may be too late.'

She looked up at him puzzled, frowning. 'What are you talking about?'

'What do you think I'm talking about, for heaven's sake? This sham of a marriage, Leonie!'

She turned cold, faint, miserably wondering if Giles was about to suggest it was time they separated, time this meaningless marriage was finished.

She swallowed, lifting her chin. 'OK, I'll leave whenever you say the word, and we can be divorced, or the marriage annulled, or whatever you like, but I'm taking Mal with me; I am *not* leaving him with you!'

'There will be no divorce,' he snarled, scowling. 'No divorce, no annulment—and you aren't going anywhere. You are my wife, and you are staying right here with me.'

She looked up at him blindly, too dazed to take in what he had said. 'But...then...I don't understand. What did you want to say to me?'

He laughed shortly, then his arm went round her, his hand flattened against her bare back, forcing her towards him until their bodies merged.

'Just that! It's time you realised you *are* my wife, and this is going to be a real marriage.'

As he muttered the words, she felt him unzip her basque, felt it give way and begin to slide down, and she gave a choked gasp.

'Don't!'

Her mind was in turmoil. What was happening? Had she given herself away tonight? Had he guessed she had fallen in love with him? He must have done, or else he would not be doing this, he wouldn't be here now, trying to make love to her!

A bitterness made her close her eyes briefly. He was a ruthless opportunist. How could he? He had suddenly seen how she felt, and was taking advantage of it without caring what that might do to her.

Her certainly wasn't in love with her. She had seen the cold anger in his eyes when he'd looked at her tonight at that party. It was the same look she had seen so many times in the past, from the very beginning, when they'd first met, when his brother had brought her home and told his family he was going to marry her.

Giles had looked at her so icily that day that it had been like a slap in the face—and from time to time since then she had seen that look again. Giles hated her. If he made love to her it would be in contempt, to hurt and punish her, and Leonie couldn't bear the idea of letting him touch her in such a mood.

It would destroy her if he did. She would have another bitter memory to add to all the others, the hurts and humiliations he had given her in the past, but this time she would loathe and despise herself, too, for giving in to him and her own stupid feelings for him.

'Don't,' she kept saying more and more angrily, trying to fight him off, trying to get away, but he was stronger, she couldn't stop him. The basque finally fell to the floor and then she was naked in his arms, shaking from head to foot, and in tears.

'I won't... Let go... I hate you,' she groaned.

'That's too bad,' Giles muttered. 'Because I'm not letting you go, Leonie! I've run out of patience.' He bent his head, and wild shock waves hit her as his mouth caressed her bare shoulder. She couldn't get away, but she couldn't bear him to see her face, read her expression, guess what he was doing to her. With a low moan she buried her head against his shirt and stopped fighting, her body quivering under the silken glide of his fingers on her skin, an exploration of her body which sent waves of heat and helpless need crashing through her.

Suddenly, his hand curled around her chin and lifted her head, forced it back until she had to look up, with a sense of shock so violent that it was like an earthquake, into his grey eyes. She had thought she knew him quite well by now, but tonight he was a stranger, his face carved into strange planes, mouth wide and sensuous, eyes glittering, his face taut with desire.

Leonie stared back, transfixed, like a rabbit hypnotised by a snake. Her heart turned over heavily, she caught her breath, shaking. Whether he hated her or not, still, there was no question about it: he wanted her, and the thought made her weaker, her legs almost gave way and she clutched at him to support herself.

'Giles, don't . . .'

'Nothing is going to stop me now,' he bit out. 'I've got to the end of my tether. I've waited long enough. It feels like a lifetime, not just a year. After Malcolm died, of course, I knew it was far too soon to even think about it . . .'

She froze, staring. 'What?' What had he just said? After Malcolm died? What did he mean, too soon to think about it? About what?

He didn't give her a chance to ask; he was talking fast, his face full of force. 'I told myself

I'd wait a few months before getting in touch again, but when your mother told me you had gone to Italy on holiday I decided to take the risk of following you out there...'

'What?' she said again, incredulously, and saw a dark flush crawl up his face.

His voice deepened, roughened. 'Yes. I followed you. I could have sent someone else—there was no need for me to go myself—on that sales trip, but the fact that it was coming up just when you were over there seemed like an omen. I couldn't pass up the chance, so I went, and when I got to your hotel they told me you were out that day, on a trip to Ravenna, so I followed you there, and saw you, and although you were friendlier than you had ever been before you cried on my shoulder and it was obvious you were still grieving for Malcolm, I was being a fool, wasting my time, so I didn't hang around.'

She was so stunned by hearing that it had been no coincidence that he had turned up in Ravenna when he did that she couldn't think of anything to say and just stared at him.

He shifted restlessly, his mouth faintly sulky. He didn't like admitting all this—it was humiliating to confess his feelings—but he set his jaw obstinately, and ground out, 'So I flew back home, telling myself it was far too soon, and I settled down to wait as patiently as I could. I thought I'd give it another six months, and try again.' He laughed curtly. 'And then I found out you were pregnant! My God, that was a shock!' His mouth twisted. 'If Malcolm had known he would have laughed himself sick.'

She winced, watching him uneasily and seeing the glitter of jealousy in his grey eyes.

'I was shaken to the depths,' he said harshly. 'I couldn't help feeling as if Malcolm was reaching out of the grave, claiming you. I was actually jealous of my own brother, even after he was dead!'

Giles ran a rough hand over his face, sighing. 'I didn't know what to do about myself, but when the first reaction died down I realised I still loved you just as much, and wanted you, and the baby was part of you, so I was going to love it, too. I saw that the baby would change everything—for one thing, it gave me an excuse for seeing you and keeping in touch. I realised that the baby might be the bridge I had been looking for—a way of building common ground between us.'

She was bewildered; he was making her see the last year in a very different light and she wasn't sure how much of what he said she should believe.

'Of course, all my threats about being his guardian, taking him away from you, were moonshine! I could never have got any court to accept my claims, and I knew it——'

'You made all that up!' she gasped.

'I wanted you so desperately I would have said anything,' he admitted thickly. 'I didn't really expect you to fall for it; any lawyer would have told you I was talking rubbish, and no court would have taken your child away from you, or made me his guardian while you were alive, but I was thinking on my feet, anything to keep in touch with you and the baby, especially after you said you were moving in with Andrew Colpitt...'

She flushed crossly. 'I didn't say anything of the kind! That flat belonged to Andrew's mother; it was meant for him, but he didn't use it at the time because he lived in London, and as he was dating Angela he offered it to me! I keep telling you this—there was never anything between me and Andrew.'

He grimaced. 'OK, maybe there wasn't, but that doesn't mean he didn't fancy you. I've seen the way he looks at you, and I know what is on his mind. I ought to! It's always on my mind when I'm looking at you!'

Her eyes fell, and he sighed impatiently. 'Don't look that way! I've finished with lies and pretences, Leonie. From now on, I'm going to say what I really feel, even if you don't like it.'

'Frankly,' she said in a husky voice, 'I'm finding it hard to believe all this! You haven't given me any idea that you...'

She couldn't hold his eyes and looked down again, whispering, 'That you...liked me...'

'Liked you? My God, I've spent most of my waking hours trying to keep my hands off you!'

Her face burned. 'I felt it made you furious just to look at me!'

'It did,' he said curtly. 'I was going crazy with frustration—of course I was angry! I had to wait so long, month after month...'

She was trembling at the emotion in his voice—if only she could believe him! If Giles loved her they could be happy, this marriage would be a real one at last. But what if he was lying?

'And since you had the baby,' he said bleakly, 'I've been afraid to move too fast, in case I drove you away altogether, but tonight I realised I was being a fool. I had to stand there and watch you flirting with other men——'

'I wasn't!'

He turned dark, angry eyes on her. 'Whatever you call it, I am not watching you smiling at Andrew Colpitt like that again!'

'Are you sure you weren't jealous because he was with Steff?' she threw at him, out of her own jealousy, and he stared at her, his brows dragging together.

'Jealous over Steff?' He gave a short laugh. 'You're crazy. If I had ever been serious about Steff we wouldn't have broken up. I ended it because I knew it wasn't deep enough to matter, and it wasn't fair to her to go on seeing her when I knew I would never feel any different.'

Leonie couldn't stop the long sigh she gave, her body trembling in his arms.

Giles watched her intently. 'Leonie?' he asked with husky eagerness. 'Were you...did you mind...about Steff and me? Did it matter?'

She looked down, her lashes flickering against her flushed cheeks, and couldn't get out a word.

'Darling,' Giles said hoarsely, and kissed her neck, her cheek, her mouth, quick, brushing kisses which made her head swim. She still wasn't sure what was happening—what had he called her?

'Darling,' he said again, his voice shaky, and she looked up at him, her dark blue eyes searching his face for clues, for a sign that he meant it, that he wasn't just using the word lightly.

He picked her up in his arms and carried her to the bed, laying her on it tenderly, as if she were made of china and might break. As he knelt beside her on the bed, his hand smoothed her fine silvery hair back from her face.

'I've waited so long for this,' he whispered thickly. 'I'm half scared to touch you in case I wake up and find I was only dreaming. I've had this dream too many times; it can't be really happening at last.'

He softly stroked one finger down her face; over her forehead, nose, cheek, mouth, jaw, gazing all the time into her eyes. 'You're beautiful,' he said. 'So lovely that you took my breath away the first time I saw you—one look and I was crazy to have you. God, if only I'd met you first, instead of Malcolm, I used to think, but I knew I was being a fool, because it was obvious you didn't even like me.'

It was true, she thought, frowning. She hadn't liked him, even before they'd met. Malcolm had told her so much about his elder brother that turned her against him. Had that been deliberate? she wondered for the first time. Had Malcolm wanted to make them enemies?

Whether he had or did not, he hadn't lied, though, had he? He had said Giles didn't approve of his dating her, and that had been true, especially after Giles met her, on his own admission.

She had known Giles was angry; she hadn't guessed why, but she had picked up those vibrations in him, and resented them. Oh, she had told herself she would go out of her way to make friends with both Giles and Mrs Kent, but underneath that she had already been arming herself for conflict—and that had been what she'd met. Outright war.

Gently, she said, 'You didn't make it easy for me to like you, did you? You and your mother made it crystal-clear that I wasn't wanted!'

'Oh, you were wanted!' he muttered, his eyes dark with a mixture of passion and laughter.

His hands moving downward, he caressed her tenderly, looked at her body with an intensity that made her bones turn to water.

'That was the trouble!' he said thickly. 'I wanted you like hell, but I couldn't show it, I had to hide it, and it was driving me crazy. It hurt. I was too jealous to think straight. I couldn't let you guess how I felt, so I went to the other extreme, and was nasty to you whenever I saw you.'

'Yes, you were,' she said, smiling, and he gave her a look that made her catch her breath, then his head swooped down and his mouth took hers.

She kissed him back, her eyes closing and her arms going round his neck, and the hunger blazed up in both of them before she knew it. She clung, her hands clenching on his back, and Giles groaned against her yielding, parting lips.

'I love you. God, I love you.'

Happiness overwhelmed her—she felt as if she were floating, her body weightless, a radiance of light around her. It was like nothing she had ever felt before; it was like being in heaven, and she barely managed to get out a husky answer.

'I love you, Giles.'

He stiffened. 'Don't say it just because you know I want you to...'

'I fell in love with you weeks ago,' she said. 'I was horrified, I thought I must be out of my mind, falling for you when I was sure you hated me. I think I must have been in love with you before I married you—that was really why I said yes, not just because you blackmailed me.'

'I was desperate,' he said, his eyes grimly contrite. 'I'm so sorry, my love. I was afraid you would go off with someone else, afraid I would never get the chance to change your mind about me—I was talking wildly, I didn't know what I was saying, I made up any crazy threat to get you to marry me. If you had talked to a lawyer you would soon have realised what a fairy-tale I was spinning you. But even if it had been legally possible I wouldn't have taken Mal away from you, I swear it. But I'm sorry I frightened and upset you; it was a rotten way of trying to get what I wanted, and I'd deserve it if you refused to forgive me.'

'Yes, you would,' she said with wry irony because she knew he might say that he knew he deserved it, but he was still banking on her forgiving him.

He looked uncertain, reading her expression, and his own eyes wavering. 'Leonie? Are you very angry?'

She pretended to think about it. 'You would have to swear you'd never do anything like that to me again——'

'I swear,' he said, too quickly, but his face was drawn with anxiety and she had to relent, smiling at him.

'Well, I suppose I can't help myself—I love you too much to stay angry with you for long.'

His arms convulsively clutched her closer, he began kissing her wildly, her eyes, her cheeks, her hair, her neck, her mouth.

'Leonie, I love you... Leonie...my darling...'

She unbuttoned his shirt and began to tug it free of his trousers, and he breathed as if he had run a gruelling race, his face darkly flushed. Desire burnt high in both of them, their bodies moving restlessly against each other, their hands touching and caressing.

Giles shed his clothes in a fevered rush, and they kissed, bodies entwined, naked and warm on the bed—and then they heard the baby crying, and lay still, heads raised, listening.

'No,' Giles muttered, grimacing. 'Not now, Mal, for heaven's sake!' but the crying got louder, more determined, and Leonie giggled helplessly.

'He isn't going to stop!'

'Maybe Susan will hear him?' Giles suggested hopefully. 'Isn't it her turn to get up, anyway?'

'Yes, but after her late night yesterday she's probably sleeping like a log.' Leonie shifted reluctantly, sighing. 'I shall have to go!'

'Must you?' Giles groaned, kissing her bare shoulder. 'Let him cry! He may go off to sleep again if you leave him.'

'And he may just yell louder, and wake your mother!' Leonie gently detached herself from his possessive arms, and slid off the bed. She put on her dressing-gown and tied the belt firmly before she went to the nursery. She hadn't expected Giles to join her, but he did, a few minutes later, also in a dressing-gown, his tousled hair brushed down smoothly again.

She was sitting on a low chair, feeding the baby, and Giles quietly came over and knelt beside her, watching with every sign of fascination.

She smiled at him, touched by something in his face, a gentleness, a warmth, that was not for her alone, but for the baby in her arms. She had wondered if Giles might ever come to resent her love for his brother's child, but the look in his eyes was reassuring.

He put out a tender hand to touch the baby's hair, stroking it back from the perspiring little forehead, and Mal swivelled his eyes to look at Giles, then shut his eyes again and concentrated on his food, his small pink fingers possessively patting the warm swell of his mother's breast.

'I'm sorry he picked the wrong moment, Giles!' Leonie whispered.

'That's OK,' he said, his eyes passionate, as he bent to kiss the white breast at which the baby fed. 'I can wait. I've waited a long time for you, Leonie. I can wait another half an hour.'

If he could be patient, so could she—but it was the longest half-hour of Leonie's life.

Fifty red-blooded, white-hot, true-blue hunks from every State in the Union!

Beginning in May, look for MEN MADE IN AMERICA! Written by some of our most popular authors, these stories feature fifty of the strongest, sexiest men, each from a different state in the union!

Two titles available every other month at your favorite retail outlet.

In September, look for:

DECEPTIONS by Annette Broadrick (California)
STORMWALKER by Dallas Schulze (Colorado)

In November, look for:

STRAIGHT FROM THE HEART by Barbara Delinsky (Connecticut)
AUTHOR'S CHOICE by Elizabeth August (Delaware)

You won't be able to resist MEN MADE IN AMERICA!

Calloway Corners

In September, Harlequin is proud to bring readers four
involving, romantic stories about the Calloway sisters,
set in Calloway Corners, Louisiana. Written by four of
Harlequin's most popular and award-winning authors,
you'll be enchanted by these sisters and the men
they love!

MARIAH by Sandra Canfield
JO by Tracy Hughes
TESS by Katherine Burton
EDEN by Penny Richards

As an added bonus, you can enter a sweepstakes contest
to win a trip to Calloway Corners, and meet all four
authors. Watch for details in all Calloway Corners books
in September.

Where do you find hot Texas nights, smooth Texas charm and dangerously sexy cowboys?

Crystal Creek

THE THUNDER ROLLS
Fireworks—Texas style!

Ken Slattery, foreman at the Double C, is a shy man who knows what he wants. And he wants Nora. But Nora Jones has eyes for only one man in her life—her eight-year-old son. Besides, her ex-husband, Gordon, has threatened to come between her and any man who tries to stake a claim on her. The more strongly Ken and Nora are drawn together, the more violently Gordon reacts—and Gordon is frighteningly unpredictable!

CRYSTAL CREEK reverberates with the exciting rhythm of Texas. Each story features the rugged individuals who live and love in the Lone Star State. And each one ends with the same invitation...

Y'ALL COME BACK...REAL SOON

Don't miss THE THUNDER ROLLS by Bethany Campbell. Available in October wherever Harlequin books are sold.

1993 Keepsake

Stories

Capture the spirit and romance of Christmas with KEEPSAKE CHRISTMAS STORIES, a collection of three stories by favorite historical authors. The perfect Christmas gift!

Don't miss these heartwarming stories, available in November wherever Harlequin books are sold:

ONCE UPON A CHRISTMAS by Curtiss Ann Matlock
A FAIRYTALE SEASON by Marianne Willman
TIDINGS OF JOY by Victoria Pade

ADD A TOUCH OF ROMANCE TO YOUR HOLIDAY SEASON WITH KEEPSAKE CHRISTMAS STORIES!

HX93

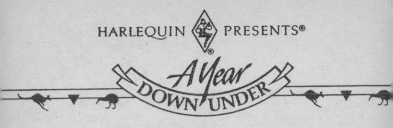

HARLEQUIN ✦ PRESENTS®

A Year
DOWN UNDER

In 1993, Harlequin Presents celebrates the land down
under. In October, let us take you to rural New Zealand in
WINTER OF DREAMS by Susan Napier,
Harlequin Presents #1595.

Olivia Marlow never wants to see Jordan Pendragon
again—their first meeting had been a humiliating
experience. The sexy New Zealander had rejected her
then, but now he seems determined to pursue her. Olivia
knows she must tread carefully—she has something to
hide. But then, it's equally obvious that Jordan has his
own secret....

Share the adventure—and the romance—of
A Year Down Under!

Available this month in
A YEAR DOWN UNDER

AND THEN CAME MORNING
by Daphne Clair
Harlequin Presents #1586
Available wherever Harlequin books are sold.

YDU-S